THE
HEMINGWAY
GAME

EVGENY
GRISHKOVETS

ИНСТИТУТ ПЕРЕВОДА

AD VERBUM

Published with the support
of the Institute for Literary Translation, Russia

THE HEMINGWAY GAME

by Evgeny Grishkovets

Translated from the Russian by Steven Volynets

Published with the support
of the Institute for Literary Translation, Russia

Cover and interior layout by Max Mendor

© 2019, Glagoslav Publications

www.glagoslav.com

ISBN: 978-1-91141-452-0

THE HEMINGWAY GAME

EVGENY GRISHKOVETS

TRANSLATED FROM THE RUSSIAN BY STEVEN VOLYNETS

GLAGOSLAV PUBLICATIONS

Contents

To L.

1

I woke up in the morning and immediately thought that I was sick. Not felt, but thought. The thought was exactly the same one you have when you wake up on the first day of the vacation, one you've been waiting for, for so long. So you wake up and think: "Why am I not having fun, why aren't I glad, where is the long-awaited joy? I must be sick!"

I woke up as if I'd been switched on. I didn't shudder, didn't stretch, didn't make any sound, I just opened my eyes. Actually just one eye, the other was pressed against the pillow. Also, I began to hear. I saw and heard…

I saw the edge of the pillow, the fabric of the pillow case, so close to the open eye. The pillow was barely lit by a bluish light. It was early, it was winter. In fact, it was still quite dark, but through the window fell an ordinary bluish morning light of the city – a mixture of white street lamps and already snowed-in yellow windows of the building across and… that of my own home. For some reason this mixture is always bluish; pleasant in the evening, but in the morning… unbearable.

I heard many sounds. They were the sounds of the city. An immense city. Obviously, I didn't hear the entire city, nor were these the sounds of some "urban pulse" or anything like that. They weren't even the sounds of the rising city – the city had long been awake. I heard how people living in my building were exiting it. They were going to work or pulling their children somewhere: the sound of steps on the stairs, the drone of the elevator, the minute-by-minute repetitive groan and knock of the building's front door. I heard how, as if with hesitation at first, and then in hopeless surrender, cars started outside, in the building courtyard. And serving as the background to all this, somewhere… a bit farther away… was the sound of the street.

I woke up. I did not feel my body, no. My head woke up. I sensed only my head. And I was inside that head. One of my eyes opened, I began to hear, and that didn't make me happy.

I so much wanted to return to dreaming. Not in a sense that I had dreamed something wonderful, but to go back to sleep. I so wanted to lose heart and call all of them, everybody, to tell them that I was sick, to lie, and cancel everything… everything! But mostly to not get up, to not turn on the bright light, to not wash or shave, to not put on socks, or anything else, to not leave the apartment jingling the keys, to not turn off the light in my hallway before leaving, to not press "1" inside the elevator, to not walk outside, to not take that first cold morning breath, to not get into the rigid, cold car… to not drive to the airport to pick up Max. But Max, my friend Max, couldn't possibly be canceled. And that meant I had to do it ALL!

And now, of all times, Max had bad timing. The kind of bad timing only an old friend of mine can have, the one who lives far, far away, who you look forward to seeing so sincerely, but who arrives or flies in, as always, at the wrong time. And those couple of days, like it or not – you give up to him. Meaning: cancel all business, whatever it may be, and get ready to talk a lot, to laugh, drink and drink some more… and talk. Sleep, of course, won't be happening for a couple of nights. This is all a good thing, just bad timing. Completely! Especially now. Because I've fallen in love. Very much! So much that it hasn't happened to me quite like this before. Never! So yes, Max had bad TIMING!

EVGENY GRISHKOVETS

2

The ride to the airport was long. There was a lot of snow. Not fresh snow, but a kind of slushy, dirty snow. There were lots of cars too. I moved slowly along the Koltsevoye Parkway. Up ahead, little red lights lit up and died down: I too kept squeezing on the brakes. The whole time, traffic in the left lane appeared to be moving faster. To the right, trucks crawled along, dirty from splashes of mud. I listened to the radio.

On the radio, music was frantically replaced with the news. They reported about some plane crash, I made it louder. All the passengers and crew had been killed. It was too early to know what caused the tragedy. The possibility of a terrorist act was not ruled out. I instantly thought of Max. Except I missed the information about the crash site. Ah – Pakistan… Disappointment brushed against me lightly. I immediately cursed myself for that, but did it insincerely, without fire or acumen.

Had this been Max's plane… It would have been horrific. Damn it – it *would* have horrific. But… What "but" – Horrific!

Except that I would have had an actual reason to be unhappy. And I would have been honestly unhappy had this been Max's flight. I could have a week of terrific drinking, of disappearing somewhere or drinking in front of everybody. And everybody would sympathize. But above all, I could call Her, right now! And say that in that plane crash, which by now she would have obviously heard about, my oldest best friend had been killed, and yes, my only friend, to be completely honest. That he is dead and I don't know what to do, and that's why I must see her right away. But Max wasn't dead. His flight was descending upon the city. He disappointed me again.

Max almost always disappointed me. He didn't move with me to Moscow when he should have moved. He stayed behind. And the bastard didn't turn into a drunk. He didn't fall. Instead, he prospered. He was involved in various businesses, and never without success. He upset me terribly when, new to the capital, I roamed and suffered, when all I needed was one thing – information from my hometown – to know that everything back there was going badly, that everyone was down and drunk, that after I left, life has stopped and everyone was awfully bored, but mainly that everyone was plagued by dreadful poverty. But no! Maxim would call me joyfully and report on his new accomplishments, how well all the friends and strangers were doing, how terrific the new restaurant was – the one recently opened not far from where I used to live – and that this Fall there has been an unearthly amount of mushrooms in the forest. He flew into Moscow pretty often; brought the usual goodies from back home. Wasted money, had fun, and on the third or fourth day would start up on how he wanted to go home. And then he would fly back home. And I hated him.

Maxim got married five years ago. I didn't come to his wedding. In general, I avoided going back home. But here was this wedding, Max's wedding to boot, which meant a real wedding. I didn't come. Max got offended. Really offended. I had never once seen his wife. Only photos. He spoke of her very little, called her often. He would just take himself off to some little corner and call his wife. After the wedding, Max did not give up on women and girlfriends… And it was definitely after the wedding that we came up with – actually Max came up with – the Hemingway game. I came up with the whole ideology and terminology. I developed the game's style and strategy. But the principle, the point of the game… that was Max's idea. I played a hundred times better than he – he often got distracted, fell apart, would not complete the game or try to quit. I would carry him, correct him in various ways. I played superbly. But he was the one who came up with it. After he got married.

Five minutes before I left the house, before driving to the airport, I spent about four seconds thinking what to wear: a sweater or a shirt. A sweater would be warmer and more practical. But what if later today I'd end up seeing Her. What if… some reason to call her would come up. There would be words, and something would work out. For that, one has to be dressed in a shirt. Most certainly! No suit and tie – absolutely not. That would look tacky and forced. Jeans, a tweed jacket and a nice shirt. Very nice. My favorite! White. Just a plain white shirt. Nevertheless, my favorite. I put it on… and went out to pick up Max.

I came out to the courtyard, went to my car, opened it. It was still dark, but already there were a few cars outside, though most had already left. I got into the car, started the engine and as soon as I did that, the lights of a car parked nearby came on at the same time. I turned: two bright headlamps were blinding me, so much that I couldn't make out neither the model of the car nor the person or people in it. I warmed the engine for a minute and drove off. The headlights moved after me, I made a turn onto the street; the lights beamed into the back of my neck and in my rear-view mirror. Though there were many cars and lights out on the street, for some time I felt only the brightness of those two lamps. Once on the street, I forgot about them. But something inside me kept scratching against the part responsible for alarm…

A shirt is a necessary item of clothing for the Hemingway game. To play the game right, one has to dress appropriately. The clothes cannot betray any forethought. It all has to appear careless and, at the same time, classy. The chosen clothes must be, in a sense, timeless. This kind of clothing is necessary to blur the signs of one's age and, thus, one's generation. Your clothes must serve to confound anyone regarding your education, line of work, income and social status. That is, your attire should communicate a kind of otherworldliness, a mystery and a hint at a certain serious, unbeknownst experience of life to anyone else who dares to play this weird game. A white shirt is the best thing to go with. And of course, no tie! Also, it wouldn't be bad to wear a wrinkled, but good, authentic jacket. As for the pants, I can't say much about that. There are many options. But the shoes… they have to be first-rate. Classic boots, sort of English, shabby, though well maintained, but without fanaticism. In other words, the shoes should be such that someone might say: "There is something to this, isn't there?"

Max has always had trouble with all this.

And another thing: players of the Hemingway game can never be called by any name other than Ernest. And during the game one should never have on his person any means of mobile communication. It destroys the image.

The first time our game just happened by itself, but gradually various rules took shape, skills developed or, to put it more precisely, a technique emerged.

One can play the game alone, but it's not very interesting. You need a partner – a spectator. Playing as a pair is ideal. By the way, if you are not old enough, don't try to play the Hemingway game.

And so, the two Ernest's set out to play. First, you have to pick some fashionable café or a club that isn't very loud. Whether it's downtown or elsewhere doesn't matter. Even if you have been to this establishment before, you must show up there as if for the first time. You should glance around, ask the bartender or waiter a couple of questions, as in, what's happening in this place? You must appear slightly awkward, but nice and smiling. Under no circumstances are you to slide over faces and figures with that characteristically wandering, seeking gaze… It's needless to say which gaze I am talking about. The eyes of Ernest must always be slightly unseeing, such eyes that every woman should want to fall into their field of vision.

Meanwhile, it is equally necessary to avert the wandering and seeking looks of women. The ladies who came expressly to be picked up, or working girls, are of absolutely no use. Very young women are best avoided as well, because they won't be able to appreciate… They will appreciate nothing. As for those visibly drunk? I wouldn't recommend them either. But there is no need to worry, you can find the right ones anytime, anywhere.

The number of women should never stop you, there can be one or five of them. That's not important. The only thing is, they cannot be with men. A small group of women who decide to get together for drinks after work are very good for the two Ernest's. Girlfriends may have torn themselves away for one night from their kids, from husbands who are well-to-do but quite busy people close to Ernest's age – they are ideal. But the most desirable object is an elegant woman who sits at the table alone, perhaps after a fight with a man or some other trouble.

The encounter happens by itself. But before it does, you must attract attention. For example, order some very complicated drink and be denied by the waiter who doesn't know how to make it. Ask for someone from the management without being rude or capricious, be kind and helpful instead. Then go up to the bar and enlighten the bartender on how to mix that very concoction. It would also be nice to somehow make the bartender and manager laugh while you yourself preserve that look of sadness. Meanwhile, your partner should watch everything that's happening with a smile. One Ernest must always look at the other Ernest with tenderness, although it's important not to overdo it and give the wrong impression.

So now you meet. Then you sit down next to the woman or women… After some time, you must take control. Though I should warn you, the Hemingway game isn't cheap. You have to order drinks. You have to be witty, but cute. For example, the two Ernest's could stage a kind of blazing, but friendly swordplay with each other.

But most importantly, you must always admire the women you meet. This admiration has to be open and pure, without pressure or a bent toward seduction. Yet, it has to contain sweetness. Genuine sweetness!

You must look a woman directly in the eyes without averting your gaze, you have to offer brave compliments, be sincerely interested in everything, everything… and at the same time, not be fussy, but slightly sad, as though wounded… wounded by life.

You have to create an atmosphere of safety, dependability and unvarnished truth. If you suddenly experience desire or temptation… You have to fight it… without concealing that fight. It means that the whole evening or part of the night must move along a certain thin edge, so that it wouldn't even occur to either party to propose exchanging phone numbers. (Max has always had the biggest problem with this.) Meaning that the better things are going, the clearer it must become that you would never meet again. Never! Yet at the same time, the faintest sound of hope must hang in the air. And at that very moment, when this thin edge is about to be breached… you must part ways! Under no circumstances are you to personally take the woman or women home. Because you will know where she or they live. And then the sound of hope will ring either fake or unduly strong. (Which is all to say that you can't vouch for Max).

You should call the taxi or hail one, help her or them inside, glance for the last time very closely into those eyes… And fall back. Best of all, if it's a rainy night or if it's snowing. Two unmoving silhouettes of two Ernest's must be clearly visible from the back of the car. You must remain still, follow it with your eyes. For a long time!

Parting right there in the establishment or walking out, or staying at the table looking sad as (she) they leave… Let's just say we have tried this. It's not a very good idea.

Night, snow or rain. Or better yet, both rain and snow.

And she who raced off in a taxi should continue to experience a sense of unrealized possibility and think: "Turns out things like this can happen! Turns out there are indeed men like this." She has to ride home on the back seat of a taxi and… smile.

And after all this, the two Ernest's should not say "Yes!" Should not shake hands victoriously. Instead, they should slowly and ruefully go home, thinking: "Turns out there are indeed women like this…"

It doesn't always work out this way. Playing like this isn't easy. But when it does work out, believe me, it's very pleasurable… Damn pleasurable! And never regrettable.

I switched to the right lane to turn from the Koltsevoye Parkway toward the airport. A sign with an arrow and a picture of a small white plane against a blue background flashed by; a sign pointing the way to the airport. My heart jumped spontaneously with joy and, just like that, dropped back down. "No, no, – I told it – we aren't flying anywhere…" The heart was rejoiced by the little white plane and the road to the airport, but it was misled… I wasn't flying away. Though perhaps I should be, doesn't matter where. It's a shame that She is here, in Moscow. Otherwise, I would at once fly to Her. I would fly to Her from Moscow. I'd call her and say: "I just flew in from Moscow. I flew to You…" Whenever someone flies somewhere from Moscow, for some reason it arouses respect and understanding, that the person came for some good reason. But when somebody flies into Moscow from someplace else – then… Well then, good for you, there will be more tomorrow, others just like you.

As expected, Max's plane got delayed. Not for long, but still delayed. With Max, things obviously couldn't go without delays. I went to look for some coffee.

How is it that there are so many people at the airport in the morning? Amazing. After all, flying isn't cheap, and yet so many people fly. There is so much junk for sale at the airport kiosks and little shops. And it's so much more expensive than in regular places. But if it's for sale, that means people buy it. They buy everything!

I drank nasty instant coffee from a plastic cup, listening to the booming announcements about arrivals, departures and so on. And all the while I kept thinking a single thought: "I love Her so much! So much!"

It was still summer when I saw Her for the first time. A big group of all types of people gathered for a party. It wasn't a picnic, but a housewarming in a suburban home. The owner's various relatives came from everywhere, a bunch of his friends, children of those friends and their relatives. Everybody knew each other very well, but I knew no one except for the host and his wife. I built that house. I'm an architect. Well, perhaps it sounds a bit embellished – architect!!! But more about architecture later. In short, I built that house. It's what I do.

The house ended up being large, with columns. I didn't like it very much, but friends and relatives were thrilled. Everyone had spread out across still undeveloped territory, as well as the house itself. Shish kebabs were about to be served. I was getting ready to bow out and vanish, since I had already given out my business cards to all the owner's friends who wanted me to build them the same house right away... same, but slightly different. She was with a man, who also took my business card. This man was about 50, tall and very tanned. Attractive, but with an overly groomed beard of complicated shape. He knew everyone in the crowd. She knew no one. Every minute, he would introduce her to this person or that. I saw her, introduced myself, said something. So did she. I didn't even memorize her name, didn't register her hairstyle or anything like that.

I left before the shish kebab. But the next morning I thought of Her, and later that afternoon thought: "I wonder, what is She doing right now?" And later in the evening: "Who is he to Her, the fellow with the stupid beard, what is it like for Her to be with him, I mean, he is boring, he must be." I thought about Her all summer and the beginning of fall.

But then, a month later, we happened to meet again, and since then I would wake up in the morning – if I'd been able to fall asleep at all – and think that I was sick. And for the whole month now I have lived as if it has all been a single endless day. The day wouldn't end. Because I kept thinking the same thought: "I can't believe how much I love Her!"

Finally, Max landed. It was announced by a loud female voice. So I headed to the arrival area. There were already people standing there, some with flowers, others holding signs, the rest with nothing. One sign read, in English, "Max Ludvigson". I thought if Max saw it, he would immediately walk up and say that it was him. But Mr. Ludvigson came before my Max. This mister turned out to be tall, with a prominent nose and wearing a green coat. He gave off a waft of tremendous foreign dullness. Then women and men in large fur hats came spilling from the doors. That's the flight, I figured. Max was the last to appear.

He was completely unbuttoned, hat and scarf in hand. Coat, jacket and shirt open midway down, were all unbuttoned. His hair was sticking out every which way, his face wasn't fresh, with a stupid little beard and mustache that I've never seen on him before. He laughed as soon as he saw me. Laughed from joy. My God, how could I live without Max!

We hugged tightly. He kept laughing. He gave off a strong alcoholic fume. Max obviously drank on the plane. He is afraid to fly.

We couldn't find my car for a long time. For the life of me, I couldn't remember where I parked it. Clearly, I left it somewhere at the airport. Otherwise, how would I end up at the airport in the first place? But I couldn't remember. I was too much in love… We wandered along rows of cars, Max lagging the whole time, buttoning up as we walked and constantly saying something…

I had met her again a month ago. It was a party to celebrate the opening of a large beauty salon. It was built by some colleagues I knew. I went there to check out yet another typical salon with a set of typically fashionable fixtures. I went to make sure that nothing interesting came of it, congratulate my colleagues on their success and to badmouth them to my other colleagues. Also, these events are always full of beautiful women, everyone is bored and, therefore, possibilities abound.

I am an architect. Meaning that I am not a state-level architect who creates "frozen music" or captures an epoch. I have no influence on the changing face of the city. I have built a dozen suburban houses. I am not the least ashamed of four of them and quite proud of one. My vision had somehow coincided with the client's desires, so it worked out. The house was featured in many architecture journals. Others were okay too, but compromised and therefore uninteresting.

Nevertheless, I ended up mastering and refurbishing a number of storefronts in different buildings. I have designed and built a whole range of shops, cafés (two cafés) and even a fitness center. I don't like doing this. The most unpleasant thing about this work is understanding – or rather, the precise knowledge – that whatever it is

I am working on, a shop or a café – will soon not be there. Meaning that after a short while, at the very place where I am now building a café, one of my colleagues will be planning some barber shop or an eyewear store. This is guaranteed! By now, I have seen how they demolish what I had built just a few years earlier. Not that I worry about it, it's just unpleasant.

And yet when Max and I were looking for my car, architecture was the last thing on my mind. What does it matter, this stupid architecture, if I couldn't even remember how and where I parked?

I don't own a Ferrari or a Porsche. For some reason, everybody thinks that architects are a big deal. Sure, there are stars, though you wouldn't know which cosmos they inhabit. I am not personally acquainted with them and have only seen them in journals. Except I don't believe that these people are building anything anymore, they just point their fingers in various directions. They can get away with it, no one will say to them: "Don't point fingers, its rude!" But that's not me. I know well which new building materials enter the market, where to get them cheaper. I am excellent at using profanities, because construction workers love that and refuse to comprehend any other words. I believe I can communicate with anybody. And I believe that I am a good man.

I used to be married… back in my hometown. By the time I moved to Moscow, I was unmarried. I almost said that I married unsuccessfully. It's just that whenever people divorce, they say that the marriage was not a success. Suppose they lived together for many happy years, but then something changed, so they parted ways. What does that have to do with success? So I won't say anything bad about my own marriage. There was much good about it, we split up more or less okay, and not without civility… from both sides. I don't want to… can't talk about this, not any more.

How can I bear it! My God! Why did I fall so in love?!

"You're looking kind of green, did you fall in love or something?" Max trotted obediently behind me, "Can you even hear me?"

"I don't like your beard!"

"It's an excellent beard, three weeks and done!"

"Shave it off right now… Damn it, where is it!?"

We finally found the car.

"Do you ever wash it?" Max opened the door with deliberate squeamishness.

"Do you ever brush your teeth?"

He covered his mouth childishly.

"I am afraid to fly! Super afraid! Sanya, I could really use some coffee, a roll and a shower." Max folded his eyebrows into a triangle, the way only he can do.

My name is Sasha.

Maxim – he is not fat, more like… stout. He doesn't get fatter, he gains weight. Meaning, he is becoming more and more the way he is supposed to be. If Max ever lost weight, no one would tell him that he was in excellent shape – they would ask if he was sick. It's hard to imagine him skinny. Max is of the breed of people who don't change. Max can be instantly recognized on school and even kindergarten photos. But this beard… this was too obscene!

We were already heading back to the city, when Max asked,

"So, the beard is no good?"

"It's inhuman! I can't imagine anything worse!"

"I thought a beard like this would be good on an Ernest."

"What Ernest!? You look more like a… Siberian torero." Again I looked straight at his beard. "It was abominable… what a nightmare!"

"Oh come on, it's just that I didn't shave for three weeks, then got up in front of the mirror thinking, figured I sort of look like one of those old-time merchants or a pirate."

"A pirate, a merchant. A Siberian gold miner, a murderer – as long as he is cute and mysterious. But this… this is some ghastly operetta character, and a drunk one at that."

"I only had a little bit."

"I don't even want to be seen with you at a gas station, not until you shave that off."

"I wanted to make you laugh."

Max turned the mirror toward his face and began examining the beard with his chin cocked.

"So I shouldn't wear a beard?"

"Oh, do what you want! But don't you see what I see? You're looking in the mirror! Are you pleased with that? I mean… take a good look, your face is a cross between a sea captain and a musketeer. And you know what a cross between sea captain and musketeer is – a fool! A pretentious fool, actually."

"Sanya, it grows in patches for some reason, I just wanted to try it… that's all. Once we get to wherever we're going, I'll shave it off. Don't worry so much."

"So let it grow in patches, it grows the way it grows. Otherwise, shave the whole thing clean, so there wouldn't be anything. But these mustaches, goatees, various sideburns are just strange. They're simply awful. Think about it, a person has a face, and thank God for that! A nose or mouth, whatever it may be, it's there and that's that. But then some so-and-so grows a mustache and fusses over it, and when he looks in the mirror – he is pleased. Understand? Pleased. If he weren't pleased, he would shave it off and change its shape. But no! He likes this exact one, and therefore he likes himself. Seriously likes himself, no willy-nilly. The more self-important and serious this so-and-so is, the better groomed his mustache and beard. But these sea captain little beards… As in, I am so intelligent, but romantic and free. All these perverted goatees… Imagine, they dye them, Max, actually dye them. Fucking Conquistadores!" As I spoke, I was becoming more incensed and drove faster. "And what about those comb over people. They grow their long sweaty feathers on one side and start brushing them across the bald spot. It's sick! Sick! And because of this, their bald spot looks like some grotesque boil with a little powder on top. I can't stand it! Just trim it short and forget it… Worst thing about it, they actually look at themselves in the mirror! And stay pleased. It's incomprehensible!"

"If I said I'll shave it, then I'll shave it. I am not arguing. You don't think I get it? Beard, no beard – same shit. I just wanted to have a little fun. But I guess jokes like this don't pass in Moscow."

Max was smiling, he wasn't upset, but for some reason I was really wired.

That's when my phone rang. Here we go. A workday giving its first signal. Except for the past month, each phone ring made my heart flutter with hope… What if it's Her? What a shame that She knows my number. Meaning, not that she knows it, but that she has it… Or had it. Either way, I had given it to her. Why did I do that? As soon as I gave her my number, right away I started to wait for her to call. It's awful! And that's on top of the fact that I also wanted to call Her. The fiery digits of her number burned inside my brain…

When I met her again, there, at the opening of a beauty shop… she saw me first. I was talking with someone and then looked sideways and saw her smile. She was already looking at me and smiling. And then… we simply said hello, recalled the time we met back in the summer. Meaning, we simply said something to each other about that time. Then somebody distracted me and she stepped away to talk to someone else. That entire time I'd use any excuse to come up to Her or the people She was speaking with. I searched the place carefully, but didn't find the man who was with her back in the summer. If he wasn't there, I had to find out who she came with. She couldn't have been alone.

I still clearly remember how casually, even sensibly, as in not without good reason, I asked for her phone number. Right away she gave me her business card, stretched it out, then, saying she was sorry, pulled out a pen and wrote her cellphone number on the other side. I did the same… And, from that very moment, was waiting for her to call.

That night she was alone. Then somebody called her, she said: "Yes, yes, I am on my way out." It happened that I helped her find her coat, helped to put it on and walked her to the exit. She looked back for a moment, made a kind of half turn, smiled and gently rolled her hand. The result was an almost imperceptible gesture of farewell. She walked out. With fine, fine little skips, she ran up to the car parked outside. A man came out, not the one from last summer. He'd been sitting behind the wheel and came out to open the front door for her. She got in, he shut the door, went back to the driver seat, and there, inside, it looked as though they briefly kissed. And left. The man was dressed in something dark, perhaps even black. A jacket or a short raincoat. It was a nice car, though not the kind that comes with a driver. A man driving a car like this had to be its owner. Of course, who else?

What a woman!

I had Her business card. I brought it up to my eyes. It had Her name!

I was so afraid it would have the name of some modeling agency, or to find out that she was a designer. It would also have been terrifying to glean something about diet food or something to do with the law. She couldn't have been a journalist. That much was obvious.

No! She worked at a travel agency. Large and impressive. She was in charge of flights. I was delighted. Airplanes – how wonderful! I kissed the business card.

Now it was possible to quickly find out who invited her to this event… to get more information…

By the time I was on my way home, I knew enough about her. She was friends with one of the owners of the beauty salon, as well as a buddy of mine who worked on the place, he also knew her a little. They said that she was very nice, unmarried, that she had an eight or nine year-old daughter. They also said that she was very, very kind.

An eight or nine year-old daughter. Imagine that. To me she seemed both youthful and mature at the same time. It was something I felt, that she was older than me. Although that probably wasn't the case. My son is ten. But she seemed older than me. Because she was so beautiful. To me very beautiful women seem… older. And she was magnificent…

I called her in three days. How I survived those days isn't all too clear. One must not call sooner than that. Even that was too soon. But I couldn't stand to wait any longer.

3

Max and I headed toward the city. It was already light out. A whitish kind of day. A cloudy winter day, matted and low-contrast. The first phone call of the day did not come from Her. It was Pascal, my amusing French friend. An architect from Paris. A very energetic and enterprising forty-year-old fellow. His father had at one time been a consul to Russia. Pascal's Russian was excellent. His accent wasn't as much an accent as it was his own charmingly erroneous, but expressive version of the Russian language. A sort of dialect that only he was versed in. Talking to him was very funny. He very much wanted to accomplish something in Moscow, arrived a couple of months before with that very goal, and got busy… So busy, in fact, that it became impossible to stop him. He really liked Moscow. But there was a bit of business he still couldn't negotiate. I promised to help, though how exactly – neither he nor I could figure out.

He called to remind me about a meeting.

"Sasha, hello, did I wake you?" He always asked this, even when called in the evening.

"No! Don't be silly!"

"We agreed to meet today. Do you still want to meet, yes?"

"Already on my way."

"Oh! But where?" Asked Pascal.

"Pascal, please don't test me. I remember when and where we're meeting."

"Good, see you soon, bye!"

He hung up.

"Want me to introduce you to a fancy French architect?" I asked Max.

"Sure! But what about the beard?"

"He is French, he won't notice! Let's go, I have to meet with him. Not for too long. They'll have a coffee and a roll there."

"Excellent! I won't get in the way, will I? I can run off to see my relatives and we can meet up somewhere afterwards. In the meantime, I'd rather change clothes and take a shower."

"Max! What do you mean, run off? I am not your personal driver!"

"That's not what I meant. I'll take a taxi."

"Max, enough. Enough with that. Of course I'll take you. But you could've told me about this ahead of time, no? This is a workday for me, you know. Work! Where do you want me to take you?"

"What is this? What's the matter with you? If you were too busy to pick me up, then you shouldn't have. No problem. Let me out, I'll get a car."

"Max!!! Where to?"

"I get it!" Max turned away. "Where are you meeting this French guy? Just go there. We'll figure out the rest later."

For a while, we rode in silence.

"Max, I'm sorry!"

Max didn't answer.

"Max, I'm telling you, I'm sorry."

"Fine."

He nodded, not facing me.

Without switching on the turning signal, I crossed over the right lane and nearly flew onto the sidewalk before stopping. As soon as I jumped out of the car and shut the door, I screamed. Screamed very loudly. A number of people turned. The scream was abrupt. It was the scream at the long end of some release. Then I groaned, leaned forward and… began to cry.

4

Pascal was waiting for me in the café on Pushkin Square. He sat right by the window and saw me as I was approaching the café. He waved cheerfully. Damn him… damn him to hell.

By then I had dropped Max off at his relatives'. We agreed to reconnect on the phone after lunch and meet up again later. Max wanted to tell me something. I know what his talks led to. We would have to move around the city and drink at every stop. And then, as soon as he took a drink, he would start dialing his old hometown friends now living Moscow. And they'd be happy to hear from him. And even if they weren't happy… they'd still come. Saying no to Max was impossible.

I felt as though I shouldn't have treated Max like this. To hell with his beard… No, the beard was awful, but the way I behaved… Anyway, it wasn't right.

Pascal and I had planned to meet at noon. I was about fifteen minutes late. Meaning, it was already a quarter after twelve and I still hadn't come up with a half-way decent excuse to call Her.

Pascal jumped and ran to me and started hugging me like a madman. It wasn't like those formal European hugs and air kisses. No, they were fierce hugs of a very happy person. Pascal did not reproachfully tap a finger on the glass dial of his wristwatch this time, as if to say, how long do you expect me to wait here? He was sometimes late too, and I'd say nothing. Yet whenever I was late, he would puff his cheeks and make some sort of gesture, characteristically French perhaps, but foreign to us. But now… he was thrilled about something.

"Sasha! Thank you, my friend. It is so wonderful! I am so, so glad!" He led me to the table where a very glamourous woman with styled hair sat, wearing something leopardesque. I didn't look her in the eyes right away, because her bust was presented as the centerpiece.

"Sasha! Meet Katerina, my first client in Moscow!"

Thank God I didn't say what nearly fell out of my mouth, because I almost blurted, "But you are definitely not *her* first client!"

"Katerina, friend of Alyosha's…"

He looked at Katerina.

"This is Sasha, I told you about him."

"Sasha," I said and smiled in whatever way I could.

"Katya," she said quietly and extended a relaxed hand, palm down. To shake it or kiss it, go figure. I shook it.

"Katerina, Alyosha's friend," said Pascal, "We are staring a very interesting project. Maybe it will come out.., magnificently! Very boldly!"

"Excuse me," I said, "Pascal, dearest, what Alyosha?"

"You know, Alyosha! The one whose apartment we went to see!"

My face retained the look of confusion, though I realized who we were talking about.

"Alyosha, the one who wants a big renovation and the mansard!" Pascal clarified.

I knew it. Of course I knew who Pascal was talking about. But I couldn't believe my ears! First of all, I was curious as to what had to happen for this Frenchman in a wrinkled, untucked shirt and old brown pants of sparse corduroy to end up calling "Alyosha" a man whose own mother probably didn't refer to him so endearingly when Alyosha was still a child. What he called Alyosha was at least one hundred and twenty kilos of living weight, without a neck, almost without hair, with enormous arms and small, forever squinted blue eyes cut into a sneaky face.

If they showed this "Alyosha" in some movie, critics would certainly conclude that this hero of ours was too much of a caricature and couldn't exist in real life. But "Alyosha" did exist. The man was from my hometown. He moved to Moscow recently, bought a huge apartment, and ordered from me, his fellow townie, an obscenely lavish renovation and then got himself a girlfriend, Katya. But even the fact that Pascal called "Alyosha" a man who back in my hometown was addressed only as "The Cycle" that was nothing. Most importantly, what I'd just heard was that my friend, the Frenchman, stole a client from me. There! Voilá! Just like that.

Spread over the table in front of Katerina were magazines and photographs, various folders. The magazines and photographs that Pascal always carried with him. When we went to "Alyosha's" he had all that stuff with him.

One time, I took Pascal with me. I still remember us hanging out at my good friends' dacha. I brought Pascal to their place. He is quite an attraction. Whenever I wanted to please somebody who was in some way genial to me, I brought Pascal. He understood very well why I took him all over, I could tell, but he never disappointed. And the one thing about him that pleased the most was the way he spoke. For example, he would report so endearingly that he was: "Tired of this drunkenly life." Or say: "I must now go metal my shirt."

So we got there, to these nice people's dacha. This nice, classic dacha in the suburbs of Moscow, with a large white wooden veranda and an overgrown garden. We got stuck there for some reason and stayed for the night. Which meant we drank almost till morning. Our host, the dacha's owner, complained that the neighbors had sold their little house, which was nicer than theirs. Sold it to some idiots, who knocked it down and were planning to build something resembling the castle of Count Dracula.

We launched into a discussion on the topic of idiocy. I, for my part, spoke of how everybody fancied themselves architects nowadays and erected God only knows what! Pascal insisted that you simply had to explain things to people, persuade them and everything would work out. I, in turn, would tell him that it was useless. Because once something was said to be fashionable, everyone would start putting up rounded turrets, until somebody else built a greenhouse, and on and on it goes. But more than anything else, there were now so many charlatans who wouldn't say a single word against their clients' wishes, nothing but dogs on a leash… But Pascal kept on about how everything can be explained and shown. I got angry and told him how we now have all these foreign know-it-alls about how this and that should be done, but who in fact don't know a thing and only take advantage of the Russian people, who live in the world of illusions and revere the Europeans. But don't you worry! This won't last long! Pascal said there was no need to stage a quarrelation (meaning "let's not quarrel" in Pacalese).

In the end, we made a bet, I promised to take him with me to a meeting with a client. I had to meet with The Cycle anyway… meaning "Alyosha". I thought: "Let him take a look at a real person and then tell me how much you can explain or show to somebody like that." I was certain that Alyosha, aka The Cycle, would not disappoint.

EVGENY GRISHKOVETS

That was a week ago. Pascal and I went to check out the apartment and the attic, which I took on for renovation and other massive repairs.

Alyosha was waiting for us in the middle of a giant space with broken windows. The walls were already demolished, but they had yet to remove the debris. The house was old, with high ceilings. Pascal got really inspired, asked me for the floor plan of the apartment and the attic and went running over the ruins of the destroyed property. We started discussing the details with Alyosha. The Cycle didn't dwell on details. None of it was all that important to him. He would take me to some house, where he liked "the way it was done". He just wanted the same thing, but better, and, most importantly, with a billiards room. A big one. The way it's supposed to be done, meaning exactly like in that other house.

Pascal would run up to the attic and back, speak some excited words about how and what could be done, and how it will be "munificent" and "spectacular"... and then run off again. The Cycle obviously heard the accent and the foreign name, and though I'd already introduced Pascal as my colleague, in about twenty minutes he asked: "And who is this?"

I said that he was my friend, a fashionable Parisian architect, who now wanted to work here.

"Sure he does," said Alyosha. "They all know where the real money is..."

I kept saying that Pascal was a romantic, but very talented, if a bit strange. Just then Pascal shoved his magazines and photos into my hands. And like a fool, I went ahead and said it:

"By the way, here... is his work."

I showed him pictures of Pascal's work in an architecture journal. One was some highly ambitious edifice. All metalwork and glass. A municipal art gallery in a small town somewhere in the South of France. Pascal had built it about four years before and got some award for it. I deliberately showed the most outlandish project, expecting to hear something like: "And they didn't lock him up for this?" or "Our guys make toilets better looking than this." But Alyosha looked attentively over the photos, took the magazine from me and started leafing. When Pascal returned, The Cycle poked a photo and said loudly, as if speaking to a deaf person.

"You did this one?"

"Yes!!! It was long ago!"

"Good man!" The Cycle exchanged glances with me and pointed his finger at Pascal, as though he were some tiny industrious creature, like a beaver or raccoon.

And that was the end of the conversation. Before we said our goodbyes, Pascal merely pushed his business card into The Cycle's hands. And for his part, The Cycle asked me in a loud whisper: "A fashionable one, you say?" "Very much so," I said…

And that was that.

Pascal's eyes were sparkling. In fact, it appeared as though the left eye sparkled brighter than the right.

"Alyosha decided that Katerina will be in charge of how things go. We are thinking about how to do the mansard, take a look."

He started showing some boldly rendered sketches. They had his signature metalwork. What he demonstrated was near savagery, even for Pascal. I couldn't fathom Katerina the Leopardesse, much less Alyosha, The Cycle, living in something like that.

While Pascal talked, I thought if what was happening to me at that moment was reason enough to call Her and tell her about it. And if it was worth telling her about, how should I tell the story: as a fun and curious episode or a story of treachery and betrayal?

"Katerina." Pascal turned to our silent lady. "Please forgive us. We are going to step a little bit away."

Katya slightly raised her eyebrows… that's all. Pascal took me aside.

"Sasha, I understand everything very well!" He said it in a calm and steady voice, having barely lead me away from the table. He now spoke, it seemed, without any accent. "What do you think, how much do I owe you for your help?"

"Pascal?"

My face must have expressed total confusion about the question.

"Sasha, I owe you for your help. I absolutely do. How much? It's normal! You help me to find a good contract, and I am paying you. Do you want a percentage or some sort of flat fee?"

"Pascal, my dear!" I said completely calmly. "Where did you learn this? Here or back home?"

"Sasha! Don't talk like my first wife, please." He said this in a tone that was somehow unmistakably Russian.

"Congratulations, my friend! This is an excellent start! See you later! I am genuinely happy for you!"

I smiled as honestly as I could, then leaned into Pascal's right ear and said in loud whisper:

"Careful with Katerina. Alyosha will fry you rotisserie style."

I stretched out my hand, he shook it mechanically. I turned around and walked out of the café. Very quickly, I came up to the car, sat behind the wheel and for at least five minutes thought about what had happened.

I had to sort this out right away. And sort it out I did, as best as I could. First off, Pascal, at the very least, won the bet. Secondly, did I actually want to do these repairs for none other than The Cycle? No, I did not! Do I really need the headache of getting Alyosha, The Cycle, all those things he wanted? No, I do not! Was Pascal deft at setting this whole thing up? Quite deft. Am I currently in love or am I not? Yes, I am. Is Pascal being fair? No, he is not. Did I correctly convey my discontent? Yes. In that case, everything is fine. I can go ahead and get drunk with Max. And isn't it great how I've manage to preserve the look of noble indignation? It's wonderful!

Pascal, what an up-and-comer! I mean, you see these foreigners walking down Tverskaya Street, not watching their step and slowing down traffic. They walk, mouths slightly agape, smiling. Seems they're all so naïve, cute, fragile. As if.

I started the car and drove, just drove ahead. I had to think of a reason, come up with an excuse to call Her. Since the meeting with Pascal went more quickly than expected, I suddenly had free time. I could do something… Such as, for instance, call Her.

5

Of course I realized that I shouldn't call. It is, after all, decidedly futile. After such calls, things only get worse. Regardless of the outcome. For example, you break down and call. Before you do, you come up with some reason, suck some excuse out of your thumb and dial the magic number… and no one answers. You weren't feeling so great in the first place, before the call, but now… it's simply unbearable! Why didn't she pick up? Didn't she hear it ringing? What if the number came up on the caller ID, my number, and she didn't want to answer? Why? Is she tired of me? Or is she busy? Or she is not alone? Why doesn't she pick up? Maybe I should call from another number, one that she wouldn't recognize.

Or she picks up, but curtly says, "Sorry, can't talk right now, I'll call you back," and hangs up. Why can't she? It's past working hours, but even if not, why put it like that? She'll call back, she says! When? The wait is unbearable. But she said that she'd call back, which means I cannot call back first. She said she would… What if she happened to be visiting somebody at a hospital or it's somebody's funeral, who knows? And what if she doesn't call back soon, how does one go on living? And what if she doesn't call back today at all, how will I sleep? How will I make it to tomorrow? Something must be done right away to leave me with no choice but to call her.

Or I call and she is glad, we speak, even make plans… And then we say goodbye, and I say: "Bye, can't wait," but she says, "Bye-bye." But didn't say, "Can't wait." Why not? Why didn't she say it? And I start thinking, thinking… And I realize that I must urgently come up with an excuse to call her right back and remove this tension, or I might lose my mind.

Or you call… and everything is fine! You have a delightful chat, make the plans, she also says "can't wait" and you say your goodbyes. You hang up and for the next ten-fifteen minutes there is happiness and solace. But very soon the solace disappears. You remember her every word… for you have nothing but those words. You pick over the entire conversation, all of its details, like tiny precious stones, and at first you're happy… but then the stones lose their luster, and there isn't enough of them. NOT ENOUGH! And you need more, more… And the need to call grows stronger and more unbearable than the last time. And you must find a reason to dial her number again.

Or her line is busy, she is speaking with someone…

Which means, you shouldn't call Her. Not under any circumstances. I realized that. Realized it from the very beginning.

I remember how happy She was when I called her for the first time…

Pascal called about five, ten minutes after I left. His voice sounded very – how should I put it? – considerate.

"Sasha! Please, forgive me. You must listen to me. I know how badly you thought of me. Forgive me, I am not as much of a bastard as you decided me to be. I will explain to you everything."

"Pascal, I…"

"I want to tell you," he wouldn't let me interrupt. "That if you don't like this, and if this means you will not want to talk to me anymore, then I will turn down this contract. I will just turn it down!"

"Aha!" I thought.

"Pascal! I can't speak right now. I am sorry. We'll talk later. I'll call you myself."

"Sashá, I urgently want…"

"We'll talk later! I'll call you back. OK? Bye!" I hung up. Good, take that! Let him suffer. Except why did I say this "OK"? What for? Somehow, it came out crudely and foolishly… I'll call him tonight or tomorrow.

Yes. So… when I called her for the first time, she rejoiced. Didn't recognize me right away, but… almost, and rejoiced. The three days – how I lived through them I'm not entirely sure – those three days since we first met, when she gave me her number, and up until the moment I called. It seemed all I did for those three days was breathe in and breathe out. But then she rejoiced – and I breathed out. I managed so easily to ask her if we could get together. And she agreed! Not that same day, of course, but in the days to come.

We met at the coffee shop on the boulevard… not too far from Chistye Prudy. I showed up early and watched her approach the café. This time I looked at her closely and thoroughly. Turned out that every time I would forget her face. I still do. Not that I don't remember it. What I mean is, I cannot hold and reproduce it in my memory. It is so beautiful that I run out of memory. And I don't want to carry her photograph, don't want her photographs at all. What's the point of photographs? I don't get it… And yet I would never want to stop taking her picture.

She came almost exactly on time. She wore a light jacket… She has wonderful taste! I very much like how she dresses! She smells so nice too! I like everything about her! I love her so much!!! Too much! Unbearably!

We've only been to that café once, and yet I can no longer drive past it. I try avoiding it. We spent no more than forty minutes there – she had tea, I had two coffees. We talked, seemingly about nothing, she laughed, and I just looked at her, thinking how much I want to take her by the hand this very minute and never let go. We sat there for forty minutes and this café became "our" café. I can no long go there; its image wounds me. And the boulevards… all the boulevards wound me. This entire city wounds me endlessly. Because She is here. And all the places in which we were together turned into epicenters of insufferable worry and alarm.

For example, she gave me her number at the grand opening of the beauty and cosmetics salon and now all beauty salons torment me and make me shudder. What's more, even the word "beauty" disturbs me in some way. And the word "cosmos", because of its proximity to the sound of "cosmetics", never leaves as much as a chance for peace of mind.

And that's how it is with everything! I found out that She worked at a travel agency handling flights – and now all travel agencies are a source of immense heartache for me… and all the airline companies too. Anything, anything that's connected to Her… And in this city, it's EVERYTHING.

I drove and thought to myself, "It's already one in the afternoon and I still can't seem to call her, can't come up with a specific reason, not to mention that I've got Max here. What am I going to do with him?" I also had to stop by another site. I was managing this so-called "construction". Meaning that I was doing yet another storefront, where certain problems had come up, and I had to stop by and have a quarrel. The crew had clearly gone lax and needed to be spurred back into action. It was too early to go there. I wasn't hungry. I'd actually been having a problem with that lately. I wasn't eating anything! Just didn't want to. Even Pascal asked me the other day: "Sasha, what is it? Have you no use for food?" I just couldn't force myself. And what else is there to do at lunch on a weekday in Moscow? And suddenly, a lucky thought occurred to me. A happy thought. "A haircut," I decided. "I need a haircut."

Back in high school, I always wanted to have long hair, but it didn't quite grow. My hair is just not that great. I never liked it. I don't get haircuts often and don't put much emphasis on my hair. But when I'm not well – not in a sense of getting sick or upset – unwell for a long time… I want to shave my head. I have done that. It helps. Not sure how, but it does. Somehow it gets easier, something is renewed. And for a while, each glance in the mirror prompts amusement, a smile even.

I'd happily shave my head this time too. But what will She think of it? How will She like it? What if she asks: "Why did you do it?" It's not like I can tell her, "You see, I love you too much; I can't bear that feeling; I'm going mad. So, I thought it would help to go without hair. Maybe that way I'll feel better."

I can't say that! So then what should I say? Anything else wouldn't be true. And how could I lie to Her? By the way, I've never once openly told her that I loved her.

I drove to Petrovka. There, amid the courtyards, is a place where you can still get a haircut from a good barber without an appointment, at least during lunch on a weekday. It's been a long time since I stopped going to places where you need to wait in lines. Those barbershops are all back home, in my hometown. Young boys and pensioners sit waiting in those lines. Everyone gets the same haircut. The radio is blaring. Plump beauticians speaking over it. They discuss everyone and everything, as if their clients don't even exist. They talk, cut hair, then shout: "Next", then take the broom or brush and, resuming their chatter, pretend to sweep around their chair. "How would you like it?" – and then back to their chatter. If they put a wooden board under my butt to prop me up, like they did when I was a kid, I would still be going to those barbershops. They'd cut my hair and tell me what a good boy I was. And I would think of myself as a very talented and wonderful person.

I got lucky. Turned out one barber was available. She eagerly took me. Tiny, thin, you might say bony, with a very expressive, sharp face. "Such a woman could drive somebody mad with love", I thought. "Probably, already has." I got very lucky with her. She was terse, attentive, and… basically, when shearing my hair, she pursed her lips so hard from focus and responsibility that they turned white. In other words, two months ago, I would have definitely gotten her phone number using the pretense that I only wanted her to cut my hair.

"How would you like it?" She asked, looking at my reflection in the mirror.

"You know… short. Take a little off the top, uncover the ears, and upfront, you know… make it nice and neat, but not too slick. And don't edge the back too much, I'm not a military officer."

She smiled, ran her fingers through my hair, wiggled them.

"Got it. Let's get your hair washed," she said.

"Let's do it, though I washed it this morning."

"Your hair is fine, it's just easier to work with when it's wet."

She washed my hair, massaging my head and pouring warm water over it. Why did I have to fall in love? Otherwise, I would be feeling so fine right now.

The moment she went to work on my hair, I began to fall asleep. I saw myself in the mirror, swaddled in this… cloth, not sure what it's called exactly, whatever it is, the thing they wrap you with in barbershops. A head sticking out from a bundle. A woman grooming the head. She carefully examined my hair and clipped it. She knew better than me how to make me look better, which length of hair would be appropriate and where. I came here because I wanted someone to take care of me.

She touched my head, turned it lightly and tilted it without force. I was falling asleep. It felt so good. My eyes closed. I saw some white stains amid the darkness. I thought, but my thinking of that thought was done not by me sitting in this chair, but by the one who was asleep.

I couldn't say that I dreamt. I wasn't exactly sleeping the way one sleeps in bed. It was a different sleep. The kind that happens when you are getting a haircut. Because sleep in a subway car or during lecture — that's a different kind of sleep. In other words, I thought… The type of thought that isn't easy to reproduce. It wasn't as much a thought as it was an idea that came in a form of desire, dream, vision, even history. But it came and went in a blink… like a flash. Like a flash of lightning

EVGENY GRISHKOVETS

in the night. Lightning illuminates the world for just a blink, but all the details are made visible. You can see so much! And you can spend a long, long time describing that moment. And that's exactly how it was. The idea came in a single moment, in its totality, in all its details… I'll tell you what I saw.

I saw…

It got dark quickly and we set up camp fires. Our battered batta-lion – an infantry battalion of an exhausted and anemic expeditionary force – was preparing to leave camp. We got orders to retreat at once. We had to retreat at night, in secret, not to attract attention of the enemy. I was ordered to stay back. We, the remaining shards of my platoon and myself, had to continue to burn fires so that the enemy wouldn't suspect anything, to make them think that our battalion was still in place. In the morning, we would confront them and try to buy our soldiers as much time as possible to leave. They couldn't move quickly. There were many wounded and even those unharmed were suffering from thirst and exhaustion.

A month before, we had broken through a narrow stretch and for some time advanced successfully. But then we got bogged down in the dunes and halted altogether. Resupplies lagged way behind. Only a few trucks were able to crawl across the sands and bring us much needed ammunition, food and water. Water was in great shortage. The last few days we couldn't think of anything but water. And so we were ordered to retreat.

I was outraged. Our scouts left two days before and had yet to return. We couldn't deprive them of a chance to get back to camp, though by then there was hardly any hope for their return. I kept insisting that somebody should stay put at least until morning. So they left me and my platoon. I was glad.

I felt great. In this world, there were no women. They were somewhere far away. But here they were hard to even imagine. The battalion was pulling out in a thin formation and disappearing into the dark. Our goodbyes were quick and silent. Shaking hands with some, hugging others. I barely had the strength to think that we'd never see each other again. Never! We were all so tired that such thoughts weren't even on our minds. Someone was hurriedly finishing a letter to give to the departing men. The final letters. I didn't write one. To whom? I wanted to write only to Her! But what could I write?

That I think only about Her. And that I will go to my death... No! I cannot write to Her like this... And if I write something cute and endearing, she'll eventually learn what happened to me anyway. She will realize that I wrote that cute and endearing letter already condemned to death. She will cry. And I don't want Her to cry. So I wrote nothing.

A strong wind gusted, raising up sand and junk and blowing across the deserted campsite. Terrible heat was instantly replaced by cold. The wind nearly tore the flame from the camp fires. The fire howled. Our flag snapped loudly over the high flagstaff. As long as we were alive – it would stay up there.

I felt good. I was tired, so thirsty and barely on my feet from lack of sleep that I didn't feel anything except a dry tongue in my mouth and heavy eyelids, which blinked slower and slower and didn't rise above mid-eye. It dulled the sharpness of seeing how strongly and unbearably I loved Her. Tomorrow – or already today, to be exact – it would all be over. I felt terrific!

I went to check and fix the fires. Then jumped into a shallow trench and staggered along to the machine gun. It was packed with sandbags. I caressed the machine gun and tapped it a couple of times with my hand. Then I pulled a steel flask out of my pocket, shook it. Inside was a little whisky. I cranked my tongue inside my mouth, moved my cracked lips, even touched them with my fingers. But I didn't drink.

I looked up. There were many, many stars. Then I looked to where the machine gun was pointing. There, in the dark, far away, gleamed the fires of the enemy camp. That's where Max went off two days ago and had yet to return. I promised him that we'd finish the whisky together. Max never forgot such promises. I put the flask back in my pocket. I stayed here to wait for him. I couldn't leave, otherwise how would I live with myself? What kind of life would it be if I left?

I sat at the bottom of the trench, right next to the machine gun. I hadn't slept the last few nights. Fighting sleep was no longer possible. "I'll get some sleep," I thought. "Just a little." At first it relaxed my bottom jaw, then my upper neck bones. My eyes started to close, my lower lip drooped. But the thought in my head persisted. Such clear and joyous thought: "It's so wonderful to have no strength, no worries! And it's great that I cannot call Her, that it's impossible. Otherwise, I'd be thinking of how to call Her, what to tell Her, to call or not to call? Isn't it wonderful? Wonderful!"

EVGENY GRISHKOVETS

My neck and jaw completely relaxed and my head fell on my chest…
It fell on my chest, and I woke up. The hairdresser giggled.

"I've got very sharp scissors. Be careful please."

"Tell me, do many people fall asleep when you're cutting their hair?"

"Yes, almost all of them," she said, looking into my eyes through the mirror. "It's alright, just don't twitch. You can sleep for another ten minutes."

I wish! I was completely dumbfounded by what I'd seen. It was so nice there. It was so wonderful! My God! What's happening to me? I must go back.

If only I could understand the mechanism of returning. Of returning there, where the remains of my battalion – in other words, of going back to that place – I would go back… and there would be not a trace of me left.

"I wonder, where were you just now? You were smiling so much," the hairdresser said in a very pleasant voice.

"Smiling?"

"Oh, yes! And moving your lips! In the cutest way. Probably had a nice flight somewhere far away?"

"Far. Very far!"

"It's so cold, isn't it? I'm so tired of winter. I would love to go somewhere warm now." She smiled, talked and kept clipping.

"How did you figure I'd gone somewhere warm?"

"I didn't figure anything. I just can't wait for summer or to go somewhere warm. But I'm guessing you just got warmed up yourself?" She continued.

"Exactly! Warmed up." I nodded.

"Don't shake your head. Very sharp scissors…"

At that moment, I saw a man in the mirror… Behind me, some man out on the street approached the large window of the barbershop and was peering inside. The window was frozen so he put his face right up to the glass. I couldn't quite make out what he looked like. A coat, nothing covering his head. He quickly looked over the barbershop and walked off, left my field of vision.

My barber finished cutting my hair. She washed it and dried it with an electric blow-dryer. Hot wind ruffled my hair and burned my scalp. "Like in the desert," I thought. It's a good thing I got haircut. A good thing!

The only thing was that some clipped hair got under my shirt collar. One wrong move while being unwrapped from that damn mantle… and all those prickly hairs were now stuck to my neck. I would have to go change my shirt and wash up. But that was unlikely to happen before evening. For the rest of the day, I was doomed to suffer terrible itching and irritation. But at least I had traveled There. It was worth the suffering.

Before leaving, I shook hands with the woman who had taken care of me for almost an hour, breathing so very close to me. Almost an hour. I was genuinely grateful. I really was!

I left the barbershop and stood for a few seconds at the door. In my peripheral vision, I saw a man in a long, dark coat hastily getting into a car. I looked directly at him, but he had already disappeared behind tinted glass. I thought it was the same man who'd peered through the barbershop window. Just then I remembered the headlight in my rear view mirror… What is this nonsense? What's the reason? Who am I to be followed? Nonsense!

The car drove off, made a quick turn and disappeared. It was a dark and boring large Mercedes. A regular Mercedes, the kind you see all over Moscow. I didn't memorize the plate number.

"Nonsense!" I thought. Once, I ran into some trouble. I was accused of stealing money. My clients, these really young guys from someplace in the Urals, got their hands on some cash and decided to open a billiards parlor. I was very inexperienced. They gave me a large amount and asked to do it the way "it's supposed to be done". They also told me not to bother them too much and when the money ran out, they'd give more.

The money ran out pretty quickly. Apparently, theirs did as well. They accused me of theft. There was all this ponderous and foolish talk, threats and scares. I was quite worried. Back then, I was just starting out in Moscow and was scrupulous in matters of money, spent days on end at construction sites… And then this happens.

They kept threatening me, and I believed them. Sure, I tried not to show fear, but it was unpleasant. They even tailed me. In short, I got some practical experience. But I've had no such experiences lately… "So it must be nonsense!" I thought.

6

A quarter after two, I couldn't take it anymore and dialed Her number. Just dialed it and that's it. I didn't come up with any excuse after all. I felt the loud throbbing of blood in my temples, but the operator's voice announced that the person I was trying to reach was temporarily unavailable. What a terrible voice! The problems this woman must have to agree to have her voice recorded for these damn phone announcements.

These voices always dishearten. They are calm and, in a way, indulgent, like the voices of psychiatrists. A person could be dying, breathing his last breath, dialing the number in desperation, and the voice on the other end of the line, a calm female voice tells you to call back later. What horrible maledictions must fly off the lips or sweep across the minds of thousands and thousands of people who hear this voice. And this is happening constantly, every second. Day and night, terrible curses fly at this poor woman – and if not at her personally, then at her voice. The life she must have!

But in reality, it's probably much less complicated. She was probably asked to record a few phrases. She spoke them into a microphone, was paid some money… And these are the consequences! Her husband or boyfriend must surely have a phone. At first, they laughed about this together, that no matter whom he called it was as though he was always calling her. But over time… it all started to go wrong. Her voice became firmly associated with something irritable… And so now they are fighting; he can't stand her voice anymore. And finally, she ends up alone. And whoever she happens to meet, they all say, "Excuse me, but your voice seems so familiar…" In short, a tragedy…

I drove, thinking about something, not about this poor woman, about something else that I couldn't seem to remember… Something alarming and discomforting was stewing inside my head. All at the same time: that man peering into the window of the barbershop, headlights shining down the back of my head, the fact that She turned off her phone and a million other things. I drove normally… making all the right turns, showing turn signals, maneuvering, braking, but I could not remember how I got to the Sadovoe Circle. And also… why I was going there. It was as though I… it's like when you are reading a book, you keep reading and realize that you've read all the letters, words and punctuation marks, but didn't understand or remember anything of what you've read, and that you now have to go back and read everything all over again. Though actually the best thing to do when this happens is to put the book away, because this kind of reading is useless.

I drove in exactly that state, and suddenly I was returned… sent back to my car… back to the Sadovoe Circle. Somebody, some woman, passing me in a small yellow car, honked and gestured expressively at me. Right away, I sensed that something was wrong with the car… My rear left tire was deflated. I had been driving with a flat for some time. It was chewed up into junk. I just wanted to curse loudly and kick the car… And that's exactly what I did. And right then I wanted to quit everything and drink, but that had to be done gradually.

I didn't have a spare tire… just didn't have one! Every goddamn day I thought I should go to a mechanic and take care of the spare… I thought about it every time I got in the car… for a month now…

I cursed one more time. It didn't help at all. The wheel could no longer be saved. I got in the car and crawled up to the nearest parking space. About a hundred and fifty meters at most. How could I be driving this whole time and not feel anything? I had to do something with the car. I couldn't just leave it like that! And so I left it. Took my scarf and gloves from the back seat, regretted that I didn't bring a hat, shut the door and left it. I'll figure something out tomorrow. "I can't deal with this right now! I can't!"

I scooped up some snow with my palm… There was a lot of packed snow on the roof of a car parked nearby. Then I knelt and began to rub the snow on my neck. It was burning with hairs stuck under my shirt collar. The snow felt very nice. "I've got to change my shirt. Take a shower and change my shirt." This thought was clear and constructive. "I should go home. Home!"

But home was on the other end of the city and nowhere near. What's more, I didn't want to see the place that I refer to when I say, "I am going home." I didn't want to see it in daylight… All the unfinished repairs, which I'd begun two years ago and now saw no reason to finish, because what I'd once imagined as home had greatly changed in those two years. "I don't want to go anywhere. Not now!" I wanted to take my head in my hands, and I did. "What a small head I have, such a small vessel! And yet there is so much shit in it!" I stood like that for a minute, and then got a phone call from Max. "Thank you. Thank you, Max!"

"Hey there! How're you doing?" He asked jovially.

"Fucked up." I answered very quickly.

"What's the matter?"

"Everything, Max! I'm without a car. Got a flat."

"Great! Then we can go get a drink right now!"

"That we will! But not just yet... I'm going to stop by the construction site, meanwhile you decide where to go. But Max, I won't really be able to go pound for pound with you. I've got another meeting later this evening."

"A woman?"

"Max, let's not get into all that right now. I am in the middle of the street, late to everything, so..."

"Sanya, hop on the metro and you'll make it everywhere on time. By the way, if it's a woman you're meeting, I won't be upset. But if not, forget my name!"

"Max, did you shave your beard?"

"Sanya," Max switched to a whisper, "I'm stuck with it. My aunt loved it. Made her so happy when she saw it on me. I can't shave it in front of her. I'll shave it later, don't worry! We'll figure it out."

"I don't want to see you with that thing. Don't even think about it! We'll speak in an hour."

I had to get out of here. I had to get to that goddamn building site. I raised my hand, a car pulled over. I looked inside. The car was smoky, filthy and hot. The driver was a guy in a cap. "Whatever," I thought.

"To Vernadsky Avenue. And I am in a hurry!"

He nodded silently. I sat down in a seat with a zebra print cover over it. The white stripes were gray, like the tank top of a very dirty sailor. I spotted a couple of small icons on the dashboard. As soon as we got going, the guy turned on music. Awful music.

"You'll show me how to get there!" He asked, shouting over the music.

"Stop the car," I said at once.

"Oh, come on. I'm just asking," the guy said very calmly.

"I said stop it!"

"Fine!" He stopped.

I jumped out of the car and slammed the door hard.

"Hey, slam it against your head," he shouted after lowering the window.

"Wash your car and yourself while you're at it! Got it? And maybe get a map of the…"

"Up yours!" He interrupted. His voice was feeble and relaxed. The car tore off the spot and drove away. I yelped something else after him… And stood there, as if spat upon. A spat upon sissy. I felt perpetually worse!

I went to the metro. The snow only briefly refreshed me. My neck started to itch again.

"I should at least take off the shirt and clean the hair from the collar. One should never go to the barbershop in the middle of the day. Or go to a salon, where they have learned how not to dump hair all over your neck. No more economizing on such things." Clearly, something had to be done. Maybe buy a new shirt or something?

But buying a shirt was a whole to-do. It only appeared easy! In fact, good shirts are just as hard to come by as… any other good thing. After all, it will end up the closest thing to your body.

Turned out it has been a while since I have taken the metro. Ah, the metro… It's neither wonderful nor awful. It's just the metro… The way it's always been.

While riding down the escalator, I tried to get my thoughts together. It had to be done. Otherwise, I was starting to really fall apart. Anxiety and anger… they'd reached their limit. A kid, about fifteen years-old, shoved me hard as he ran past me on the escalator, so I grabbed him, cursed him up and down and pushed him away. What for? My nerves were shot to hell.

That's when I launched into a meditation. The kind of meditation that always helps me in moments of inexplicable alarm. I had to locate the source of anxiety, localize it, acknowledge it as such. And even if it's impossible to remove or fix it, you still begin to feel better.

In that case: What's shaking me up? In all, everything is more or less fine. I currently have two projects. Everything is OK with one of them… What's with the OK again? What am I, some kind of cowboy…? I've got to start getting rid of these OKs. So, everything is fine at one of them, the other is in trouble. That much is clear. The man at the window, a car waiting at my door and a general sense of surveillance were all disturbing. But that was nothing. What surveillance? Why would anybody watch me, of all people? Alright. Now Max. Max? What about Max? Max is Max. All is well there. The car? What about it? I'll make a call in the morning and they'll tell me what to do about it. The car is literally nonsense. So what isn't nonsense? That my house has been a mess for who knows how long? Yes. That bothers me. I don't like that. I like everything to be tidy, clean and pressed. I like my car washed, so that various junk doesn't pile up in it and the trunk contains only a few necessary items, no boxes, packages, magazines, which I planned to give away three months ago. I love my books and music in proper order, my desk uncluttered and its drawers nearly empty. I love tossing out different junk – greeting cards given to me or those which I myself planned to give and never did, business cards of people I couldn't remember, booklets, newspapers, travel guides to different cities I'd visited and so on. When I throw away junk, living becomes easier. When I wash my car, it drives better, when I take care of my footwear – my health improves. But now everything was in a state of total disarray. Even unfinished home repairs can have some sort of structure, but now… shirts in need of washing and ironing were hanging all over the place. Books, some papers scattered about… basically, everything! Not to mention dust… which covered the car as well. And the bathroom… a horror!

From time to time, I would find people to clean my house. They were maids or women that had moved in with me for a while. But only I myself could achieve the ideal level of cleanliness. I did that… very rarely. If I went too long without shaving my head, I would clean my house. I really wanted to do that right now. But I had absolutely no strength.

"Fine," I kept thinking, "Right now I can't handle dealing with the clutter; that bothers me. But it's understandable! No reason to get all worked up about it. In any case, it's fixable. Am I upset about Pascal's trick? I suppose not. In fact, he probably helped. In all honesty, I didn't want that contract anyway. Pascal is alright. Besides, he wants to apologize. Everything is fine with that. So then what's causing me to feel so rotten? The shirt with all these hairs? Yes! Seriously! I've got to deal with that pronto. And she turned off her phone. There is my main source of distress. I am not well. Not well! I've got hear Her voice! Soon! Right now!"

I pushed my way into the subway car. It was packed. "It's also thanks to the winter clothes," a thought flashed in my head. "It'll be easier in the summer. It always is. But something has to change by summer, or else I won't live long enough to see it." I closed my eyes and even let out a barely audible groan. Then my eyes opened and I saw people's heads at eye level.

We stood tightly pressed against each other. Heads were swaying, the train ran quickly through the tunnel. I saw these heads. Through the window at the end of the train car another one could be seen. There, it seemed, people were swaying harder. And to them it probably seemed the other way around. "There, amid all those heads, is my head," I thought. "And what in the world is happening inside that head? If there was equipment that could catch the energy of stress, my head could be detected from outer space. It could even be seen through the earth's crust, underground, where the subway lines ran. Right now, I think I am hurting more than anyone else. There can't possibly be so many hurting heads in one place at the same time. There can't be! It'll fry the wires! My God! If I could manage to kiss Her, it would probably blow up a power station somewhere in Uruguay or New Zealand. I have to sit down. I have to sit down right now!"

I had a roughly twenty-minute nonstop ride ahead of me before reaching my station. I really wanted to sit down, and when a seat became available, I went for it decisively and sat down. I saw a stout elderly woman in a coat and mohair beret with a hairdo underneath rush toward the same seat. She held a large bag. She used this bag to move people out of the way. Having observed my maneuver, this bag lady (if you allow me), shook her head reproachfully.

"I don't care!" I decided firmly. "I don't like this bag lady, don't want to give up my seat for her!" I shut my eyes so that I couldn't see anybody.

"Shame on you! Nearly killed everyone here for it," said the bag lady. "And now just sitting there, pretending not to see anybody. No shame, no decency!"

"Fuck yourself, you taint," I thought calmly and with determination. "It's not like I'm obliged to give up a seat to you. I've been giving up seats since childhood. Childhood is over! Besides, this was one nasty bag lady. A spiteful one. I needed it more now. Scream all you want. I won't move, and that's final!"

I forced myself not to think about this or get riled up. There were three guys to the right of me. I heard their voices and what they were talking about. They spoke loudly, with a strong Moscow lilt.

"I'm not getting the car, what's the point?" One of them was saying. He must have been straining not to use foul words in public, because his speech was somehow decelerated. "Tolyan doesn't like lending it to me just like that. That means I have to wash it and drive you all around. You'll be drinking like fish, and I…"

"Check it out, you need the car anyway! We'll drop by tomorrow morning, buy everything…" the other one was saying. "How much beer can we carry with us? Won't be enough for the weekend! And out in the country, where are you going to run for beer in the cold? We'll take everything at once, and that's it. Then pick up the girls and go. Once there – drink all you want! All day long. And on Sunday we won't be drinking either…"

"I don't want to ask Tolyan for the car. He fucking whines…"

How I envied these guys! They were planning their weekend. I didn't envy them because they were getting ready to "drink like fish" for a couple days in some village, but because they had weekends off. They actually had weekends! Worked the whole week, made it to the weekend, drank – didn't drink, went fishing – or not… doesn't matter. They had weekends! The last time I had a weekend was probably in my hometown. A long time ago!

And who would give me a day off now? Who would give me a day off from what was happening in my head? Who was going to give me a day off from Her? Nobody! And even if somebody did, how could I take it?

I must call her immediately. If she agrees to meet today – that's one thing. If she can't today, can't for sure, then right after the construction site I'm hooking back up with Max… and going drinking!

What a wonderful thing it is to drink with Max. Especially before. Back when I broke up with my wife, we'd go drinking pretty often. At first, I was no match for Max's excesses, but later… even surpassed him in many respects. Initially, a strange feeling would get in the way, as in GO HOME! Meaning that at some point an internal brake would activate itself, the feeling of freedom and joy would start to disappear. So I'd have to tell myself: "You do not have a home where someone is waiting for you, where you have to say something to somebody, where somebody will be saying something to you. There is no home that you must, if possible, be back to before midnight. There isn't anyone who is waiting and worrying or sulking. NO ONE! Go ahead and have fun!" But the fun would somehow wane by itself. And melancholy, or something like it, would creep up. This had gone on for a long time. Then it went away. But I did have weekends, to be clear, even while I was married. Some weekends...

I really enjoyed to get drunk with Max on a Friday night on a whim. Things always unfolded in the same fashion. We'd go out for beer, eat, then get ready to go home, but... I could never quite do that. So we would move on to someplace else. Just after eleven, I would always call home.

"Already on my way, dear. Max and I got stuck here. It's Sergey's birthday, but..." I tried to speak as quickly as possible before being interrupted. And I thought I spoke in a completely sober voice.

In response, I'd always heard either: "Don't try too hard on my account!" or "I get it!" or simply silence, and then a dial tone. In any case, I could never speak to that second reply. So I would get mad and start to drink without stopping. I'd get home around three in the morning, sneak across to the sofa, knocking over chairs. I would feel terribly in the morning. No one would speak to me. I would feel sick, call Max. He'd feel even worse. We'd chat a bit on the phone, make plans to meet in some tiny smoky restaurant, where everything was somehow brown, and each evening a musician named "B-Flat" would sing and play. This restaurant was exactly half way between my house and Max's. Everything was so close in our hometown. By the time I showed up, Max would already be there, sitting with a glass of beer.

Summer weekends were especially nice, when you could sit outside the restaurant under umbrellas. And in my hometown there were never that many people out at two o'clock on a Saturday afternoon.

So I would walk to meet Max down the street that wasn't as much familiar as it was completely etched in memory. The sun would get in the way of seeing, and tiny cracks in the pavement would get in the way of walking. The brain inside my head would feel like a kind of pipe organ. And it didn't matter what I looked like a that moment.

EVGENY GRISHKOVETS

And we'd sit across from each other in silence.

"Turns out it's so hard to go through life with your head raised high and proud," said the slouching Max. He'd had only a tiny bit of beer while waiting for me. My beer mug had barely a centimeter more than his. He'd order beer for both of us and waited. Max always issued sad witticisms when hung over.

"Max, I asked you not to order me a beer. It's already gone flat and warm," I grumbled.

"Be quiet, will you? What sort of a person are you?" He would take his mug, I'd take mine...

So tasty! So I'd drink another small beer, and Max would drink a large one. After that, they'd bring out a hot salty hodgepodge with a shot of ice-cold vodka. We'd drink up and dig in. Another few minutes and life would start to return. Sun, large leaves on trees, shade from the umbrella, the sounds of summer, children on their bicycles... And the thought, which makes a heart leap so high with joy: "We have a whole night ahead of us and tomorrow is Sunday! Bliss! And the summer is only just beginning! My God! How wonderful! The weekend!"

I rode without opening my eyes. I was tired. Very tired. My head was bent, chin resting on my chest... It's not clear how long I'd slept. Ten-twelve minutes at most. Woke up because I slumped over the nearby passenger. Good thing I did! First of all, I didn't miss my station, and secondly, I sucked drool oozing from my lower lip back up to my mouth. I wiped off my mouth in a swift motion and looked around wild-eyed. Wild because of what I'd seen in those ten-twelve minutes... or rather, not what I'd seen, but where I'd been.

I stood there, feet far apart. Eyelids heavy. So sleepy that for a couple of minutes I seriously questioned whether it was possible to keep my eyes open with matches and how this might be done. The sailor and I were the only ones left on the bridge. The sailor had just reported for watch duty, but could also barely keep to his feet. There was absolutely no point in peering into darkness. You couldn't see a damn thing, yet we were stubbornly doing that. The storm subsided. We'd been rocking for three days, but it was better now. The whole time I had barely slept. Had to spend the whole day in the engine room. The mechanic and two drivers had hardly gone up to the deck. The old engine simply refused to work. I'd go down to check on them periodically. But what could I do to help them? During the storm, we barely manage to stay on course without capsizing. Now that the storm had waned, the mechanic announced with pride that we could give it twelve knots. But what's twelve knots when for the last six hours… I counted every hour!

It's been already six hours and still no signal from Max. His SOS was first picked up by the Norwegians, who set out on a rescue but reported thick ice around the search area and opted not to move any further for reasons of safety. In all, fourteen vessels set out to rescue Max. The Danes were going to scramble together two planes and had even begun to prepare them, but the weather turned so bad that flying was out of the question. The storm descended and raged for more than 24 hours. Rescuers were swept every which way. Most hurried to come back.

But the SOS continued to get through. We'd lose the signal, then pick it up again. I was absolutely certain that Max was still alive and holding on. What happened to his ship, nobody knew. He just suddenly transmitted a distress signal. What's more, it came from where no one had expected him to be. How did he end up there? And what now? We alone were crawling to his rescue at the speed of twelve knots, even though by then we might as well be sending out an SOS of our own. But this was six hours after he went silent.

I told the helmsman to stay on course and decided to go back to my cabin. I passed by the galley and looked in. Inside, the cook was sleeping in a sitting position. I woke him, not without regret, and asked for coffee.

"Six pieces of sugar. Bring some up to the bridge too," I said. "And give him something to eat. Let him eat, then he'll fall asleep."

I took a large tin mug with hot brown muck. I knew what kind of coffee *this* was. Coffee in name only. I had to drink something hot and sweet. I took a big gulp… and almost screamed… so badly I burned my palate and even my esophagus. My eyes filled with tears and I felt the skin peel off my palate. This kicked sleep aside, but not for long. I stuck a finger inside my mouth, gathered burnt skin from the palate and wiped my hand on the sou'wester. The senses dulled.

The Danes, the Norwegians, the Swedes, they all warned us about thick ice. But we were simply too tired to be afraid. Besides, thick ice or thin, what's the difference? To this ancient soup bowl of mine it was all the same. In other words, we were going to drown anyway.

I pulled up my hood and came out to the forecastle. There was a lot of ice on the deck, the railing iced over beautifully. The wind blew

EVGENY GRISHKOVETS

cold, not very strongly. "Dark!" that was the only conclusion that that my sleepy brain could draw. "Somewhere out there, in the dark, is Max."

At that moment, I was called up to the bridge. They caught another SOS. Turns out we were on the right course all along.

"Some instinct you got," said the sailor.

The Radioman, the helmsman and myself, all we could do was smile. I reported the good news to the engine room and asked to increase speed. The mechanic grunted something and turned away absently, as though he was somewhere a thousand miles away instead of here. That's when I realized that I had to lie down for at least a half hour. I went back down to the cabin and sat down on the cot. For a couple of seconds, I thought about the bottle of Brandy locked in the ship's safe, but decided that I simply had no strength. And besides, those waiting for us there, out in the dark, could use it more... "Max will be so happy," I thought and, without lying down, just leaned back against the bulkhead and instantly fell asleep...

I was awakened by the feeling of toppling over, reeling sideways. I also felt saliva drooling from my mouth. I sat up straight and opened my eyes...

There weren't that many people left in the subway car. The bag lady was sitting right in front of me. There were glasses perched up on her nose and she was reading a paperback book. When I looked up at her, she wet her finger and turned the page. "Touching," I thought. "She probably takes the metro all the time. And I no longer do. Good!" I also thought about the dirty car with a flat tire and the mess in the trunk. And suddenly I remembered the vision that I'd just returned from. Once again, I thought how good I felt there! So simple and wonderful! I have never experienced such clear, coherent and consistent visions. "These don't seem like dreams," I realized. I had to think about this. Because there, inside... inside of whatever it was that I kept seeing, everything was lucid, exact and crystal clear... What's more, it was easy! I, who sat in a car of the Moscow metro, yearned so much more for the "I" who was out in the cold sea... or in the desert. "The salvation, it's out there!" I realized. "The salvation!"

7

I walked out of the subway onto the street and immediately dialed Her number. Then immediately hit cancel. My mouth felt foul. I didn't eat a damn thing the whole day and, on top of that, fell asleep on the subway. Even over the phone, I didn't want to speak with Her with my mouth so disgusting.

I bought some gum from a kiosk. Chewing, I started to dial, then canceled the call again. How could I talk to Her while chewing?

I checked my watch… half past three! Taking the metro was faster after all! Although it seemed slower.

I had to eat something. Just grab some food and force it down. The empty stomach was making me dizzy. But I wasn't hungry at all. The thought of chewing and swallowing something, whatever it may be, was sickening.

I bought a bottle of kefir and quickly poured it into myself. "It's healthy," I thought and laughed to myself. "What's healthy? What for?" Two years ago I bought myself an exercise bike. Now it stood amid the mess in my bedroom, its presence communicating to the mess a certain youthfulness, wellbeing and a hope that determination and good sense will eventually arrive and take charge in this room. How many times have I seen these exercise bikes sitting in garages, closets, attics and dachas… and still I bought one. A useful purchase only in that after this exercise bike appeared in my house, I stopped thinking about the need to go jogging in the morning, or go to the skating ring, or lift weights. It stood next to the bed as if to say: "It's all pointless!"

After buying it, I pedaled for only three days, respected myself a lot and went up to the mirror more often than usual. But whenever Max came to visit, he'd sit up on it, still wearing his coat or jacket, and start up with me…

"Sanya! Say, what are these digits? The kilometers I'd covered or what?" He'd ask, fingering the display.

"No. That's the calories you burned. And here – the meters," I'd explain patiently.

"Sanya, but you realize that this is all bullshit, right? The Americans tricked everyone with these calories pretty good. Good for them! I should get one too," he blabbed, pedaling faster and watching the digits flicker, "Does it help?"

"With what, Max?"

"You know, generally…"

"It does. Generally."

I was walking from the subway to my construction "site", constantly slipping along the way. I don't like Moscow when it's got all this stale snow, slippery ice and cars covered in dirt. It feels as though the city is tired, as if Moscow has shrunk in height, bloated into heaps of snow and pressed down by the dark sky. It wasn't even four o'clock and already it was getting dark and the lights already on in many windows. And in some of those windows they've been on since morning… "We all are tired, tired together," went the sound in my hand.

I didn't have far to walk. Before coming inside, I stopped at the storefront sign that said "construction". It was quiet. That meant things at the "site" were indeed going badly. What a joy it is to approach a construction site and hear knocking, humming, loud voices. "Time for a serious talk," I realized. But before stepping inside, I dialed her number.

I was afraid to hear that voice again… Not Her voice, but the voice telling me to call back. I afraid… simply afraid. I always experienced that fear when I dialed Her number. But then the seconds, required for the inscrutable event of two phone numbers connecting, passed… then came the long ring tones. First… second… third… And She picked up!

8

I cannot reproduce Her words. Though it feels like I remember her every word, everything that she has said when we met or over the phone. I remember each intonation… But I will not reproduce or repeat Her words. I just can't!

She picked up the phone delighted to hear from me. Right away, she said that she had an important meeting and had to turn off her phone. She figured that I'd tried calling and explained everything. Amazing, isn't she!

I, of course, asked how her meeting went, she said that it went well… After She asked how I was doing, I quickly told her everything… About my friend Max visiting, and how I would love to introduce them; told her about the car and the tire; about problems at one of my sites.

"Oh, and also my friend Pascal, remember, I mentioned him before… This Frenchman, the scheming romantic. Remember, I told you about him, this naïve, very vigorous French guy," she, of course, remembered right away, "so turns out he isn't so naïve". I laughed. "I'll tell you what he did when we get together. It's very amusing…"

Then I asked if she wanted to meet later that evening, that this evening after work would be great, even if for a little while. I said that I would meet her anywhere.

She told me that she couldn't say for sure if she would make it today. She wanted to see me as well, but there were some complications having to do with her daughter. She said she'd call me back. But I told her that I'd call her myself in an hour. She laughed. Laughed in a good way. Yes! Intently, I felt not just better. I felt great!

"Now I can go and have my fight," I thought and stepped inside.

When a job is going well, it's very loud, yet there isn't a whole lot of trash. Here, it was the exact opposite: silence and everything cluttered with garbage. Wires were hanging down everywhere. In other words, things were pretty bad. There was nobody inside the larger commercial space of this future store, and it was cold. Sounds were coming from the hallway. I followed them. It smelled of cigarette smoke and food. From the back room came laughter and voices... there were smells coming from there as well.

Some sitting, others on their feet, there were six young construction workers in dusty green overalls: among them Borya the foreman, a big, thick-browed burly fellow in blue building gear, and my assistant, Grisha, a nice, sprightly guy, who very much wanted to be like me and tried to imitate me in everything. When I realized that, I started to excuse him more often and reprimand him less.

As soon as I walked in, everyone fell silent. Grisha's was the only hand I shook. I greeted the rest of them with a nod and glanced over their faces. There was instant tension. Obviously! They knew it was coming. They were ready for a confrontation.

The room was quiet. It smelled bad, there were unwashed cups and a grimy kettle on the table. A calendar displaying three bikini-clad asses was pinned to the wall. Everything in there spoke of decay and sabotage.

"Grisha, step outside with me for minute!" I said to Grisha. "Excuse us, we'll be right back," I turned to the rest of them.

There is nothing scarier to a construction worker than being addressed politely. It brings out a sense of guilt. Not always, but often. I exploited that.

Grisha and I went off to another room.

"So what's going on here?" I asked.

"Problems! It's Pasha, I transferred him to another site, he had a son five days ago. He told me about that. I gave him a couple days off. So that same day he bought all this stuff, figured... After work hours, of course. Meanwhile, the owner stopped by with some friend of his. That was the only time... Nothing really happened. The guys were tipsy, got excited when the owner showed up, even poured him a shot, you know, to make him feel welcome. Anyway, he started yelling at them, then at me. Said he wasn't going to pay, that he wants to replace the crew. Basically, threatened us. Pasha got upset."

"Whether he pays or doesn't, that's something for me to worry about." I said rather sternly. "Grisha, what's the real problem here?"

"Well... That's the problem."

"What is?"

"The guys," Grisha vaguely pointed back toward the room where the workers were gathered, "they would like their money."

"What money? They already got their advance. Now we need results, then they'll get the money."

"They say that we should at least get some money for Pasha, so he could celebrate the birth of his son."

"Haven't you done enough celebrating?"

Even as I spoke, I realized that I was wasting my time explaining this to Grisha. These tough men, working stiffs, especially when they're together, have such an ability to plea for your conscience, to press upon your sense of right and wrong. Grisha shrugged his shoulders.

"What is this, a strike, or what?"

"No, not exactly… It's just that the owner, he didn't exactly act right either." Grisha became completely disheartened and could no longer look me in the eyes. "He didn't want to hear anything, said he'll only speak with you."

I'd obviously managed to neglect things. That much was clear. The owner of this store was a fairly neurotic young man, would check everything ten times in a row. But that was normal. Worse than that was that he became convinced that he was overpaying me. He constantly brought in his expert-friends to the site, who told him what he wanted to hear – that he was being seriously deceived. Still, even this kind of behavior is business as usual. I just can't stand the whining. Still, money is money.

Somehow, this site wasn't working out from the beginning, so I distanced myself from it in some faint-hearted fashion. Pasha, who'd just had a son, was a nice guy who has worked for me for a long time. Borya – a decent foreman, too. Same for the rest of the workers, I didn't know all of them. Just another crew. But problems piled up and everything has gone awry. Grisha wasn't keeping up, the client, meaning the owner, was all nerves, calling constantly… And me…? I have fallen terribly in love! And that was all.

This cycle had to be broken. The guys were already working slowly and poorly and now halted altogether, clearly preparing to make some kind of a statement. I am well acquainted with this collective demagoguery, these peasant grievances and searches for justice. I don't like this. I had to go see them, even though all I wanted was to go and see Her.

I came back to the room, in which seven resentful men, all united in their resentment, were waiting for me.

"And? So, what now?!" I couldn't come up with anything more absurd and helpless. But I had to start somewhere. "Who are you striking against here? This won't stand! You haven't worked for two days. Which means no weekend off this time. It's that simple. To say nothing of drinking on the job, that's a separate discussion. This type of..."

"Until we get paid for what's already done, and until we get an apology, we're not doing any more work," said a large guy with blond hair. He was the only one sitting, everyone else stood. I haven't worked with him before. The way he said it…. let's just say he's been preparing to say it.

"That's a strong statement!" I responded. "What else?"

"We need to get Pasha back and give him a small raise!" Said a tiny, wizened fellow. His overalls were the cleanest. I've known him for a long time. A fine professional, decent guy. "The man had his first son. We should show some kind of respect."

"Respect? Raise? Really?" I cut him off abruptly. "Sure, a raise! For drunkenness, for being rude and sloppy. A raise, certainly!"

"He's worked hard until this incident, and I wouldn't say that he was rude," Grisha intervened.

He was standing just behind me. The truth is that at that moment he was feeling worse than everybody else. He stood, as it were, between me and the crew. Grisha felt guilty all around, but his butting into the conversation was neither here nor there.

"Drunkenness on the job is disgusting! And I won't tolerate it. You, Grigory, know this well. I'll be having a separate discussion with you," I said, not even turning to face him. "If you are incapable of managing the work, then don't interfere!"

"We drank after work. The man had a son! Can't we have a drink after work?!" said the blond one.

"He is the problem," I realized.

"Have a drink? Be my guest! I don't care! But on the site, while wearing work clothes – that's pure filth! I don't care if he had trip-lets – you don't do this." I was looking the blond directly in the eyes, he looked right back and smiled arrogantly. "You'll be reprimanded for drunkenness and sabotage."

"This is our workplace," said the blond, without taking his translucent eyes off me. "We work here and we can celebrate… you know, congratulate a friend." He emphasized the words "our" and "we".

"This workplace was given to you by me. And I decide what I allow or don't allow here, understood?!" I emphasized the word "I". And I do not allow drinking!

I already decided to fire this tow-haired twerp and was deliberately ratcheting up the exchange. I needed a victory.

"Say thank you that we didn't cripple this… owner of yours." He continued. The rest stood in silence. Which means they agreed with him. "The things he said to us, people ought to answer for those kinds of words."

"I have nothing to thank you for! You personally!" I pointed my finger at him. "And I don't give a shit who said what to you here. If you are here, wearing work gear, then you have to work, not spend two days hanging out. Understand? I'm definitely firing him," I kept thinking as I spoke. "You got drunk, and there can be no excuse for that, nothing here…"

"Now listen, what're you harping on, 'drunkenness', 'drunkenness', got nothing else to say or what?" the blond lost it. "Great!" I thought. "That's it, he is out."

"You better leave words like 'now listen' at home. Save them for your parents, because they clearly didn't raise you right." He was downright stunned. I purposely touched on the subject that's "holy" for these pathetic blowhards: parents.

He got up abruptly, nearly jumped. His face turned spotty. The right cheek lit up with an irregular shape of flush. "Looks like the map of Africa," it quickly crossed my mind.

"What, you want to hit me?" I said very calmly. "Just bear in mind that nobody will help you with that around here. They're not exactly in accord with you. My colleagues and I," I made a roundabout gesture, "have worked together for a long time and have never stooped so low as to have fist fights. Isn't that right, Boris?" I behaved Jesuitically. I was destroying the very core of their collective indignation. Was it manipulative? Yes! But what was I supposed to do?

"Well…" Borya mumbled in response, flitting his eyes.

"In other words, young man, you're fired…"

"Don't call me young man, understand?" The blond said completely helplessly, but with some militant poise.

"I have nothing else to call you. We'll never see each other again." I turned to Grisha. It was painful to see him like that. "Grigory, please pay this… man for the past two days. Let's not be miserly. Take back his work gear and tools. Look, you know what to do. I'm sorry, Grigory, I don't doubt your professionalism, but…"

"Fucking dolts!" Said the blond to everyone but me, hurriedly removing his overalls.

"Grigory, why don't we step outside. Let's not bother the young man while he's changing." I said to the dumbfounded Grisha. "Boris, please wait a minute… Everyone else, hang on," I turned to the foreman, who nodded eagerly. "Grigory and I will be right back."

"Grigory, I have two questions for you. Did you drink with them? And where did this character come from?"

"I toasted to Pasha's son one time with the guys," it seemed like Grisha was about to faint. "Forgive me, please. And this guy… he is my relative from Tver. Just out of the army. I didn't know him at all. Relatives had asked… He's not so bad…"

"He is very bad!" I interrupted. "Maybe he'll get better, but I'm not a pedagogue and civilizing him is not our business. As for giving work to relatives, it's a thankless act. But worse than that is that you drank with them and are now forced to defend them. For that I'll have to reprimand you as well."

"Sure! I am not objecting!" Grisha rejoiced. "I am not denying anything…"

At that moment, the blond walked past us with a gaping stride. He wore a black jacket and a knit hat. Before leaving, he turned around and, speaking to Grisha, said: "Thanks!" Then he brusquely walked out and slammed the door.

"Guys, now listen," I said to the crew as soon as I walked back into the room, "We'll definitely get Pasha back, don't you worry. What's the real trouble here? Seriously now, and without hysterics."

"Sasha, you see…" said Boris, "The things he said to us, this client of yours… After those things, we don't exactly feel like doing anything for him. All the guys here, they're alright. So they had something to drink… We explained everything to him… And he… just started screaming. And who is he to scream at us like that?"

"Alexander, he really did say hurtful things," Grisha said to me with conviction, "and threatened us! And he wouldn't listen to me at all."

"He would listen to you if you didn't drink like the rest" I answered. "But since you did, Grigory, your position is rather weak. And responding to rudeness with rudeness is the last thing one should do." I took out my phone. "Would you please remind me our client's number..."

I dialed the number and pressed the phone to my ear. Everyone silently waited for what would happen next.

"Hello, good afternoon! Evgeniy Lvovich?! How are you! Yes, this is Alexander!"

He recognized me and right away started speaking something very quickly. But I had seven pairs of eyes watching me.

"Excuse me, Evgeny Lvovich! I am currently at the site and would like to tell you the following: if you have complaints about the quality of work, the timeline of its execution or about my people, please express those complaints to me. This isn't the first year these men are working with me, and I won't allow anyone to insult them and order them around. Remember, you are nobody to them, understood?!"

He must've collected his thoughts and began squealing something into his end of the line. I pulled the phone away from my ear, winced and winked at Boris. Everyone smiled approvingly, shuffling from foot to foot.

"Evgeny Lvovich! Evgeny Lvovich! Stop! Shouting at me it is pointless! So is threating me! You already owe me for the completed work. But if you continue to speak to me this way, I'll take my people off the site!" He tried to interrupt me. "Evgeny Lvovich! We'll talk this over on Monday, but unless you adjust your tone, there will be no discussions. Good bye, take care." I hung up.

It was a total victory. "It's a shame that She can't see me right now," I thought.

Everybody started speaking at the same time, a relief came.

"Grigory, don't worry! This Evgeny Lvovich isn't going anywhere. Bring Pasha back, wherever he is," I said in a low voice, then turned to everyone else.

"Guys, you do not work for this cretin," I showed them the phone as if the client, Evgeny Lvovich, was inside the device, "you work with me. So let's deal with all this junk. As long as we have so much trash all over the place, no good work can be done, as you well know."

"Yes, Sasha, will do. We'll take care of it right now. And it would be nice to get Pasha back here tomorrow. No one else will handle the electrics around here," said Borya. He was happy now that the tension has eased.

"Alright guys, you've had yourself a weekend. So you'll go without one for now. But I'll let you cut out early for today. And please get rid of these asses," I pointed to the calendar on the wall. "Grigory, help your colleagues pick a decent calendar."

"Grisha is the one who put it up," said the little neat one. Everybody broke into laughter.

I got my wallet and pulled out several bills.

"Another thing, I will not give Pasha any special promotions because of his son," I said, "Let his wife and mother in law do that. But chipping in for a present – like you said, that's only fair, I suppose."

"Grigory, please walk me out, would you," I called to Grisha, "Alright, fellows, that's it for now," I shook hands all around and headed for the exit. "Don't ever drink with the workers. Never! Let this be a lesson to you, Grigory. See you tomorrow. Goodbye."

I gave Grisha a firm handshake and walked out. It was almost dark outside. I quickly took out the phone to call Her. But first I checked my watch. No, it was still too early to call. Fifty-three minutes have passed – I said I'd call in an hour. So I dialed Max.

9

As soon as Max picked up, I immediately said: "Max, I'm sorry, let me call you back a little later. Five minutes or so. Alright?" and I hung up.

Some twenty meters to the right of the exit – meaning, the entrance to the place I had just left – that same Mercedes was parked. What the hell. "How is this possible? I took the metro. Who the hell am I to be followed?! What's happening?!" I thought in a blink. I wouldn't say that I got scared, not at all. But it was discomfiting... very much. I had a strong urge to walk up to the car and ask directly: "What exactly is the problem?" Perhaps that's what I should have done. But I did it differently. I turned right and headed towards the avenue. The headlamps lit up and the car moved from a standstill. I walked about twenty five meters, stopped, turned around and blatantly stared at the Mercedes that was crawling after me. I was able to make out the shape of just one person behind the windshield glass. The glare from the headlights was blocking the view and the side widows were tinted. Abruptly, the Mercedes picked up speed, drove past me, then stopped at the red light, switched on the right blinker and, as soon as the light turned green, shot onto the avenue and sped away.

This was starting to get serious. I had to think about this and figure it out. For some reason, I became very concerned for Her. I was struck by an unbearable urge to call her, to make sure that She was alright and to warn Her. But warn her about what?! I dialed Her number... She answered right away.

Instead of the usual "hello", she laughed. Then said that she could synchronize her watch by how precise the timing of my calls was.

My God, how lucky I am to have fallen in love with Her! How nice it is to be with her, how soothing. I instantly felt more relaxed.

She was laughing and in excellent mood, said she'd stepped out of the office and therefore could talk freely. It made be both thrilled and discouraged. I had nothing to say to her. I mumbled something and once again asked about getting together. She took about three seconds to think and said that the only chance she'd have to meet was after work. She had nobody to leave her daughter with. She worked till seven and we would have half an hour to get coffee together at a small café next to her office. I was thrilled! Terrific!!! Wonderful…

"Wonderful!" I said. "I'll be there at five minutes to seven. See you soon. Can't wait! Goodbye!"

She also said "can't wait!!!" My worry regarding the dark Mercedes diminished and faded away, as though I'd been examining this worry in the binoculars and flipped the binoculars the other way around. And just like that, everything has become small and toy-like.

Max called me himself.

"Where've you been?" He grumbled. "I am starving over here."

"Max, do you need me to spoon-feed you?"

"You said we'd meet up to get something to eat. Right? I'm sitting here like a fool waiting for your call."

"Max, don't blackmail me. You should've just eaten. We agreed to meet up. Meeting up and eating are not the same thing."

"Sanya! Then what the hell do I need you for? How can we hang out if there is no food? At least when you're eating, you are not spouting like you always do. Not with your mouth full. Must be because in Moscow no one listens to you, so you…"

"Max, anyway! Did you decide where you want to meet?"

"Sanya, which one of us is a Moscovite? You know everything better than I do. If I pick something, you'll start wincing and whining. Let's go to the trendiest place!"

"There is no such thing as the trendiest place in Moscow. Can't you get a bite to eat without me? You're like a child, honestly."

"I want to go to a restaurant. One waits and waits to come to Moscow, to go to a good restaurant. It's Moscow, Sanya! Moscow!!! It's a shame to waste time on some crap," he kept moaning.

"Max! I don't have too much time to linger in restaurants. What is it now?" I knew what time it was, but for some reason glanced at the watch anyway… (Once, I conducted a little experiment. Whenever I saw a person… any person, check their watch, I would immediately come up and ask them: "What time is it?" Everyone, without exception, would check their watch again before answering.) "Let's see, it's five now, and at eight I have a meeting… A quick meeting. After that, I'm all yours again. And now, let's go to a Georgian restaurant. The one on Ostozhenka. What do you think?"

"Excellent! I'm on my way," I could pretty much hear him jump up. "I'll be there in half an hour."

"The hell you will with the traffic there!"

"I take the metro, Sanya! Remember? The metro?" Max hung up.

Whenever it was actually important to show up on time, Max had always been late. But to a restaurant he'd definitely show up even ahead of time and manage to either hook up with somebody or order everything, or both.

Max called back in six seconds.

"What's the name of that restaurant exactly?" He asked.

"Genatsvale. It's around..." I didn't get a chance to finish, when Max hung up.

I breathed in dark, cold, winter air. Breathed it deeply into my chest and exhaled white steam. I felt good. Moscow! It's something, isn't it?

I walked up to the edge of the avenue. An inevitable pile of slush had collected there. But this time I was watching my step carefully... like I usually do. I like good shoes and take good care of them. This time, however, I was carefully looking around. What was I trying to see? It's not clear. Anxiety and a certain caution have made my vision and hearing sharper. I should say so! By then I had practically no doubt that I was being watched and followed.

Cars were going past me. Lots of them. I raised my hand. A taxi pulled over.

"Evening. Ostozhenka please?" I asked and examined the car. "Looks fine," I thought.

"With pleasure," said the driver, a large man with long hair, shaved face and big round glasses. He wore a light-color sweater. He was smiling.

"Do you know how to get there?"

"I do! Imagine that!" He answered. "I've had the occasion of going over there about..." he made the face, as if counting something in his mind, "a million times!"

I got in the back and off we went. The driver turned on the music. Not too loud... comfortable. The stereo system installed in the car was a good one judging by the quality of sound. He put on some type of jazz. I didn't understand much about it... about jazz. For me it was all a single endless and meandering composition. But this seemed pleasant. I narrowed my eyes, which made the city lights and lights from cars all around split into elongated rays. There I was – a taxi, crawling lights, jazz, the smell of an automobile, being followed… America!!!

"Does the music bother you? Should I turn it down?" The driver asked. "The only thing is, I won't turn on the radio. I don't listen to the radio."

"Everything is fine. I like it. Thank you," I replied.

"If you smoke, please go ahead. But absolutely no radio." He had a very low pleasant voice.

"Thank you, I don't smoke. Why do you dislike the radio so much?"

I thought the following answer would be about how he can't stand listening to that terrible music they play, or that the news is always negative, so why listen when life itself is already so awful. But I heard a very different answer.

"I don't like the radio, I don't listen to it. I worry too much. I get this feeling that I'm missing something. There are so many stations. Their sheer number worries me. Even though all those channels are more or less the same. The news is pretty much the same, the music… Still, it worries me somehow…" he spoke slowly, calmly. It was obvious that he has been driving people around Moscow for a long time. He is asked something – he answers. If not, he stays silent. By the way, Moscow used to stress me out, too. Until I learned Moscow well, I was anxious, couldn't sleep, was afraid to miss out on something. But I have since learned this city… not completely, but I would pass with a solid B. I'm calmer now. No jitters.

"You like jazz?" I was now curious to ask him other questions.

"Not really, but I listen to it. Can't go totally without music. But there is so much music out there now that I worry about that too. But jazz – it's just that, jazz. Besides, it's customary to think of jazz as serious and complicated music. People who listen to it are smart, complicated… So they treat me accordingly, as in, here is this man, listening to jazz – must be a serious man. So they don't smoke without permission or leave a mess."

"What about when you drive alone, do you also play jazz? Or do you have a favorite music, just for yourself?" I was genuinely interested.

"I never turn off this jazz. It's playing, not playing – doesn't matter. It's good music! Don't think I'm being coy. I know about jazz, a long time now… and the stereo I installed in this car isn't shabby. But I don't bring my favorite music to the car. What do I need this emotional strain for? Right? But if I were to tell you seriously about music, not just shooting the breeze… Favorite music is the kind… the kind you love... You know what I'm talking about? The music you love doesn't come without that strain." He turned to face me for a moment. "That's why I play jazz. Meaning, music for those who are done with love!"

"Excuse me, are you from Moscow?" I asked for some reason.

"Oh yes, I am a Muscovite."

"And how old are you?"

"Not old, but older than you," again, he turned quickly and smiled.

What a cool taxi driver! I like guys like this. Genuine taxi drivers who have spent a long time driving their own cars along the streets of their own city. There aren't that many of them. I mean genuine ones. Those who genuinely love and understand the people they're driving. Meaning us, passengers. I don't mean love us for real. They drive so many people back and worth. They know so much about people! Taxi drivers – it's not like they're romantics or urban angels. I am absolutely sure that this very driver, with whom I was having such a nice time riding, if I were speaking with some foreign accent or were a slightly drunk Siberian fool, he'd charge me so much that my head would spin. Surely, he would know where to find prostitutes and how much they charge. If you're careful, you could learn from him where to get drugs in this city. He knows it all. He has driven so many rude people across these streets, people who showed no respect to him, belittled him, behaved atrociously, that I myself would have lost all faith in humanity. He has seen so many accidents, crashed cars, bodies torn apart and smoke still coming off them, that anybody else would have long turned into a burned out cynic or hysterical idiot. He's seen his city in all kinds of weather, all seasons and under all the lights. He's spent so much time on these avenues and streets, sitting in traffic jams, waiting for various official cars with special escorts, swerving away from scumbags and jerks, fools and halfwits, who all pour out onto these avenues and streets daily. If I'd suffered even an infinitesimal share of all this, it would be enough for me to curse EVERYTHING once and for all.

And yet he keeps driving…

I remembered when I first felt like I could orient myself in Moscow.

For many years, I didn't like Moscow. Whenever I traveled here for business, or just passed through by train, it would frighten and upset me. I couldn't tell from what end the sun rose, couldn't sense distances. Everything was far away in Moscow. I would dip into the metro or, with skepticism and apprehension, let taxi drivers displace me about Moscow. Here, in this city, the most frightening thing was to lose a scrap of paper with a phone number of some relatives or friends, who could be of some help or with whom you could crash and spend a night. It used to be so easy and satisfying to rag on Moscow. The clothes I wore whenever I came here always seemed wrong for the weather. Either too hot or too cold. And then I moved here.

I remember driving my own car on Moscow streets for the first time. By myself. And I was terribly amazed. There was nothing to fear. Nothing at all! It was so amazing – I was driving through Moscow. No one was pointing fingers at me, everything was fine. Nothing special. I was so stunned by that feeling that I made a couple of loops along the Garden Ring, and then spent half the night driving around. Everything that weighed on me and oppressed me suddenly vanished… Little by little, I began to pick up on the city's halftones and clearer sounds. It was as if I have removed a space suit and was amazed to discover that I could breathe here. And that there were people. Lots of people…

I was warm in the taxi and I felt like I was starting to sweat. So I unbuttoned my shirt and loosened the scarf. My neck was burning. I couldn't keep myself from scratching it. The driver noticed it and cracked open the window.

"Thank you," I said. "Exactly what I needed."

Cool air and the noise from the street felt comfortable… But my neck…

"Is something bothering you?" The driver asked, more formally this time.

"Oh, it's nothing. Went to a barbershop at lunch, the hair got under my collar. I can't stand it! But what can I do, I'll have to live with it for the rest of the day."

"Oh yes, it can be a real nuisance, I know," he said rather indifferently. "If you like, I have some aftershave. You know, with my type of life, I always have a set with me."

"I wouldn't mind. Thank you!" I accepted it not out of politeness, but because the itch was really getting to me. The driver took out of the glovebox a kit, which contained a razor, shaving cream, toothpaste, toothbrush and an aftershave lotion. I rubbed the cooling, burning liquid on my neck – just one of life's many pleasurable sensations!

"Great guy," I thought. I had to figure out how much to pay him... meaning, how much to tip. That's the hardest. How to appraise, with money, his care and assistance. It's not like he was trying to help me just to bump up the fare. He just helped. Maybe he just liked me. How do I express my appreciation in monetary equivalency? It was important not to get it wrong. I shouldn't give too much – he could get upset, say that I was paying him for sincere help. But paying a standard tip would be just as wrong – I had to show that I appreciated his style.

"By the way, take this, might come in handy," he said and handed me something...

"What's this?" I wondered.

What I was holding in my hand was a thin, very smooth fabric.

"Some lady left it here, a while back. Take it, you can wrap it around your neck, it'll be like cravat or neckerchief. The kind poets wear," he said in his calm, pleasant and some highly mature manner. "And then throw it out, when you don't need it anymore."

"Oh, no! I couldn't possibly," I handed it back to him.

"Go ahead, take it. I'll throw it out anyway. It's silk, so I can't use it for dusting. It's been sitting around here for a long time," the driver turned on the light. "Look! It looks nice, doesn't it?"

I was holding a small silk kerchief. Blue, with small white polka dots. I smelled it; the scent of perfume was still discernable. For some reason, I thought of Her. The idea that it could be Hers. My heart started to beat not faster, but harder.

"I don't know. What if she wants it back?" I said languidly. I did like this neckerchief, I wanted to take it, but I had to keep up appearances.

"I've been driving it around for a long time. Take it. You know how much stuff people leave here? I could dress half a Moscow."

"Then maybe you better give it to some woman." I wouldn't let up. "It's nice and definitely not cheap."

"What woman?" he said and turned around. "Come on! Didn't I tell you, I listen to the music 'for those who are done with love'. Get it?"

At eighteen minutes to six, we pulled up to the restaurant. I stepped out of this nice man's car. I could not ultimately decide how much to tip him. I ended up paying just above the usual. I parted with him awkwardly, ended up unhappy with myself.

I looked after his car as it drove away. I did it rather ritually. It was my way of expressing gratitude. I lucked out with that man. For over thirty minutes of my life, I lived intensely and interestingly. A second after he disappeared from view, I realized that I left my gloves in his car.

10

The city around me has taken on a different form. It now contained danger. My gaze was no longer dispersed, pointing slightly forward and down. My gaze now pierced the street far ahead. At first, I scanned the landscape in front of me and then analyzed the details. My gaze rushed forward, attempting to search behind corners. This way I could look all around. The familiar Mercedes was nowhere in sight. I entered the restaurant.

I had no doubt that Max was already there. The first thing I did was check my coat, get the numbered receipt. Number 53. It told me nothing. The figure was unremarkable, devoid of any numerical magic. Then I went to the restroom.

I removed my jacket, hung it up on the stall door, walked up to the sink and glanced in the mirror. I liked myself. Over the last month, I didn't so much lose weight as grow haggard. Tired face, eyes glistening with exhaustion, white shirt – very nice! I pulled up the sleeves to wash my hands and discovered that the cuffs were nearly black. Of course! The car, long-unwashed, the subway ride, a visit to the construction site… Moscow…

I unbuttoned the shirt down to my navel and began rinsing the collar with the wetted hand. There were lots of tiny, tiny hairs so I kept wetting my hand and scooping them out. Then I buttoned myself almost to the top and tied the driver's gift around my neck. The smooth silk spread over the neck like some release from torture. I didn't work it up into some flamboyant bun. It came out nice. My look instantly became not so much contemporary as otherworldly. I smiled.

But the shirt was, unfortunately, no longer fresh. I tilted my head and smelled under my armpits. The image in the mirror instantly seized to be flawless. I spread my arms, looking into the eyes of my reflection. Then I rolled up my sleeves a couple of times to cover up the dirty cuffs, put on the jacket and tried to catch the scent of perfume from the silk scarf. I picked it up, looked in the mirror for the last time… And managed to stay pleased after all.

Max was sitting at the far end, near the window, facing the entrance. He saw me as soon as I walked in. He saw me and laughed joyfully.

He looked fresh, his hair combed, but that stupid beard was still on his face. As I approached the table, some eight steps away, he was still laughing and pretending to hide from me under the table.

"Please Mister, don't hit me," he said loudly, laughing and blocking his head.

"Max, come on, what are you, a clown? Didn't I ask you," I knew he wouldn't shave that beard. There is no more stubborn person than Max. At least I haven't found one. "Come on up, stop horsing around."

"Sanya! Look at you! You've always been the most stylish," that was Max reacting to my neckerchief. "What do you say to the Hemingway's today? By the way, I took your criticism seriously." He picked up a burgundy leather briefcase from the chair nearby. He unclasped it and produced a pack of disposable razors. "Here," he said, "I can get it rid of it any time."

"That's some briefcase!" I couldn't help myself.

"Swanky, huh?" Max took the briefcase by the handle and rotated it in the air, displaying it from all sides. "Ran out to the store and bought it while waiting for you to call. Wanted to get a cap, bought a briefcase and flashlight instead." He took out a small flashlight, which you could either hold in your hand or fix to something and use as a lantern. Max started flashing it in all directions, including into my eyes. "Not bad, eh?" He asked.

"Not bad at all!" I said in all honesty. "Let me see."

It was a very clever flashlight. Small, heavy, nice to handle. A flashlight. Right then I thought I should buy the same one for Her. Surely, it will make her happy.

I haven't given Her any gifts yet. For the life of me, I couldn't figure out what to give her. Not in a sense that it may or may not suit her, or whether she'll like it or not, but as in… what's the nature of our relationship? What can I give to her other than flowers?

Even flowers weren't so simple. I don't understand a damn thing about them. I've consulted others, then realized that the best thing to do is give roses. But these roses… there are so many kinds! The first time, I picked out very small, almost white roses. They had a slightly greenish tint. She liked them. She really fancied them and asked the waiter to put them in some water while we were having coffee… it was in the café in

Pure Springs. Then there were the baby-pink ones… three large roses. But they were seized by the frost while I carried them, or maybe they just sold them to me no longer fresh. Anyway, they were dying right before our eyes. It made her sad, but she took them anyway and told me that she was going to cut the buds, pour some water in a cup and let the buds float in it… The third time, I bought her a single flower in a pot. It was made up of large leaves sticking out of the soil like a frozen explosion. They had white veins and the name of the plant was in Latin and complicated. I bought it because of the veins and the name.

We only met four times. For the fourth time, she asked me not to bring anything at all. Meaning, no flowers. This time (it was last Saturday), we met at the food court of a large shopping mall. She was the one who picked such a strange place. She was very sad, excusing herself from the table periodically to talk on the phone. She kept stepping away, I heard her speaking with somebody in nervous gestures. I didn't ask. I felt so awful. I didn't want to let her out, back out into her life, which of course was, and is, full of all manner of everything…

I didn't ask her about anything, but then she suddenly took my hand. For about three minutes, the planet stopped spinning. She said that she had been dealing with a difficult situation involving a man with whom she'd lived with the last two years. She said, evenly and directly, that she never loved him, but that he came into her life at a time when she really needed care… She let him care for her… Also She said that there were many good things about those last two years, that he was a good man, but that he wanted assurances, meaning… a family… and so on. She never wanted that with him, though it would have been more logical and practical to accept. She even wavered…

And then she said something that made the paused planet spin out in two swift revolutions, sinking several small islands somewhere in the Indian Ocean.

She said that she almost agreed to his proposal, or rather his continuous onslaught. She'd simply run out of arguments and strength to reject him. Arguments in defense of her own self-interest. And then suddenly there was me!

She said it just like that. Then promptly got up, asked not to go after her, put on her little coat… and quickly left. Of course I didn't do as she said, but I had to pay for the coffee. I left five times as much money as I owed on the table and rushed out to find Her. But I couldn't. She

EVGENY GRISHKOVETS

wouldn't answer my calls. I dialed her number about a hundred times that evening… And just about died that night.

I came back home. For a long time, I stood by the wall, then for a long time sat rocking in a chair. I roamed corner to corner without taking off my shoes, then lay on the floor for several hours and groaned. That night I experienced a terrible starvation for oxygen, I had no skin. I have never endured anything more horrible in my life.

Once, long ago, I was a student in school, served in the army, suffered. When I returned from the army, there was much of everything to life… When I moved to Moscow, I very much suffered from loneliness and doubts. I was terribly upset by my inability to be with my son, my tenderness for him wounding me to tears… But it was all nothing comparing to what I felt that night. I realized that I did not have any life experience. All that I knew, all I was that capable of – it was all useless and wouldn't help.

That night I learned that love was neither happy nor unhappy. That it was unbearable in either case. I lay on the floor and understood that I didn't know WHAT I WANTED. What do I want? I curled up into pretzel, right there on the floor next to my bed, and fell asleep. In my sleep, I pulled the pillow and blanket off the bed. Woke up at noon. But I didn't feel any better. I woke up as though I was switched on at exactly the same spot where I have been switched off. Like I said, it was as if I was living a single endless day. A day that wouldn't end.

I woke up and, without much hope, dialed her number. She answered. Answered… and spoke as if our date at the shopping mall never even happened. And just like that, I was delighted and revived.

The most agonizing thing about being in a state like that are the transitions from hope to despair, from certainty to doubt and back again. These jumps constitute the bloodiest parabola one could imagine.

In any case, a flashlight was the most appropriate gift for her today. It was ideal in many respects. A flashlight – it's useful, and beloved since childhood by boys and girls alike. A flashlight – its joy and romance. A flashlight sets no expectations and can delight Her and her daughter.

"Max, let me buy the flashlight from you!" I said.

"What? A rare thing like this? Give it back!" Max reached for it across the table.

"I'll buy you one just like it. Tomorrow! Alright?" I wasn't giving it back. "I need it now, understand? Now! And where am I going to find one?"

"No, Sanya! I can't. I need it myself. I bought it because I need it." Max was smiling, happy with himself. "Why do you need a flashlight today anyway?"

"I just need it, that's all."

"You want to give it to a woman!"

"Leave me alone, will you? I'm telling you… I'll buy you one just like it tomorrow."

"Where will you get a thing like this?" It was now clear that Max would give up the flashlight. He was just showing off. "Sanya, come on, you want to give my flashlight to a woman?"

"You guessed it! Asshole!" I felt myself slightly blushing.

"Must be a nice woman! You don't give a flashlight to some bimbo. A flashlight is a… Oh, just take it!" Max waved me off.

"How much do I owe you?"

"What? How much of what?" Max expressed confusion.

"What did you pay for the flashlight?" I asked Max, mocking him right back.

"A kick in your ass! Got it?" He displayed indignation. "What did you pay, he asks? Where did you learn how to talk like that?"

A flashlight! What a brilliant gift. How did I not think of this myself? I was glad, very glad!

"Tell me about her," Max asked suddenly.

"She is nice, Max. Very nice!"

"That's it? I want to know more about the woman my friend is about to give my flashlight to."

Max guessed it. I really wanted to tell him about Her. Or to be more precise, not tell about her, but talk about her… I wanted to talk about Her all the time. That there is this amazing woman. Down to earth, real, mature, beautiful, smart, sophisticated, and so on. It seemed that there was no more important topic than Her and everything about Her. I needed to talk with someone about Her…

"No, Max! I'm not telling you anything else about her. Maybe later. Not now," I said more than seriously. "Thank you for the flashlight."

Then we ordered food. I really wanted a drink, but I couldn't. Not before I met with her – I couldn't. For some reason, I was certain that when we met, I would tell her that I love Her.

We ordered quite a bit of food. Max couldn't stop poking his finger in the menu. He refused to drink without me. We got mineral water. I asked for coffee first. I only got to drink coffee at the airport in the morning. Atrocious coffee.

Neither the smells, nor the scenery of people dining, nor the names of dishes on the menu returned my desire to eat. Even though I loved Georgian food so much. Especially the cold appetizers. All these sophisticated blends of nuts, cheeses, beans, mint… garden greens. Georgian food is the real thing. Diverse, multifaceted, with lots of possibilities. In other words, quite appetizing!

But right now I did not want to eat.

"Max, why did you really come to visit?" I asked in the process. Meaning, in the process of Max consuming his food.

I pinched a bit of this and that. But Max was eating as usual, with appetite. When he finally pulled himself away from the food, they brought me a third cup of coffee. I fidgeted, thinking only about leaving the restaurant and meeting Her on time. I still had plenty of time and there was no need to be anxious, but I was anxious. We blabbed about this and that. Actually, it was mostly Max. It was just blabbing. Nothing special.

Here is the chat between me and Max that took place at the Georgian restaurant "Gentsvale":

Max: So you're not going to tell me about this woman?

Me: Max, I won't just tell you about her, I'll introduce you.

Max: Aren't you scared?

Me: Jesus, Max… knock it off.

Max: Alright, alright. So I suppose that means you're in love?

Me: Stop it! What are you talking about it?

Max: You are in love! Lucky man. Good for you, Sanya. I met this lady recently. You know, young, quiet. We were both on the same page. She knew I was married. Back home everybody knows everything about everybody. Like I even have to tell you! Which means, we couldn't see each other openly. It's a small town. We spent a week talking back and forth on the phone, then one night I ask her out, on

Saturday, to this restaurant just outside this city. You wouldn't know about it since you left. It's a nice place they put up. So anyway… I ask this lady out one night. Everything is perfectly clear between us. You know what I mean? I pick her up downtown, we're driving. She is cheery, laughing… Everything is fine. I reserve a table for two by the fireplace. We get there, sit down for dinner. Chatting about everything, the mood is great. She is in law school. Smart girl. Great sense of humor. We drink champagne, have something to eat. In other words, the evening is just beginning, and we've got the whole night ahead of us. I'm thinking to myself: "With a girl like this, I can keep talking till the next morning." And then she suddenly leans over and says to me in a whisper that today is… not just another day for her. You get my drift? That time of the month… the female situation? So I looked at her for a minute and said: "You know what, sweetie, there is nothing else for us to talk about. That's all. We're done talking." We finished our food, drinks, I took her back to the city and went home to sleep. What, why are you laughing?

(I really was laughing.)

Me: Max, you're a piece of work! *(I kept laughing.)*

Max: What do you expect? I took a second to play the whole thing out in my mind. I mean, what do you think would happen? Say we'd talk some more, make out, hug… right? I doubt we'd even do that since you couldn't finish what you started. Remember? We talked about this. About physical contact, all the bodily movements and then the quick romp, that all of it is nothing compared to foreplay, which is more important. It was you, by the way, you were the one who claimed this. That all the talking, the hints, the doubts – like, is it going happen or not happen – touches and glances – that's where the real pleasure is… That if we could do away with that final sparring – all the better. Hey, what are you cracking up about? You were the one preaching this stuff. Remember how you said that before the physical contact, everything is veiled, that we're all so talented and witty. But as soon as the deed is done – that's it! Anatomical details creep into view, you start thinking about work, get sleepy and so on. Makes sense. But as soon as it became clear to me that the ACT was not happening… You know? *Definitely* not happening. Any inclination to be witty or talented vanished at once. And any interest in listening to her vanished too. Even though before she broke the news,

EVGENY GRISHKOVETS

everything was wonderful. And by the way, when I was settling the check for our dinner and champagne, I regretted spending that money. And I regretted the evening, because it was a total waste. What's more, I felt chagrin… that I was let down and cheated.

Me: Is that right? Because I tell you, you actually lucked out with this girl. Otherwise, imagine going through all these pains for her half the night and then she tells you about her problem when you're already all steamed up. Now, that's chagrin for you! You'd puff up all your feathers, and at the last moment… Poof! An insurmountable obstacle, as it were, now stands in the way of your passion. An impenetrable barrier…

Max: Go ahead, keep laughing. But you'd do exactly the same thing. Don't even argue. Don't pretend like you wouldn't, I won't hear it, won't believe you anyway.

That was our chat.

We were served by a very courteous older waiter. He was displaying, as I saw it, excessive zeal and attention. It annoyed me, but Max liked it. This fellow quickly analyzed the situation and went to work on Max. He could tell that he wouldn't get much out of me. He didn't like me.

Soon I would have to leave for my date. Max and I planned to keep in touch and then get together again somewhere downtown just after nine…

I could stay for another fifteen minutes. We asked for the check. That's when I thought: "Where is my coat check receipt? Where is my 53?" I checked my pockets, looked around the table. Max and I lifted and put back down all the napkins and plates. Then we carefully searched under the table. Again, I checked my pockets and emptied their contents on the table, Max even turned his briefcase inside out. His own receipt, with that flashy number of 33, was there. What about mine?

Our waiter watched us carefully. And when I stood up, arms akimbo, and expressed total perplexity and a refusal to search any further, he approached and asked with a strong, genial Georgian accent:

"I am sorry, but I'm guessing it's you who left his ticket in the restroom. It was returned to the coat check. Please, do not worry!"

I got really angry. He saw us looking for at least five minutes. Why couldn't he come up and tell us sooner…?

We sat back down to finish our coffee, got our check. By then I was hopped up. My nerves shot to hell. Besides, I was already tired.

After we got the check, we had another discussion.

Here is my second talk with Max at the restaurant "Genatsvale":

(The waiter handed the check to Max. Max looked at it, nodded faintly and pulled out his wallet.)

Me: Hang on, let me see.

Max: Why?

Me: I have to.

Max: Not, you don't!

Me: I said let me see!

Max: Today, I'm paying.

Me: No, we'll pay together.

Max: Let me pay…

Me: Let's not argue about this, alright?

Max: *(looking at the check)* Its nothing at all, hardly worth talking about.

Me: Even better, why argue over it?

Max: Yes…

Me *(I grabbed the check from Max's hand)*: Nothing? Are you crazy?

Max: It's fine.

Me: What do you mean fine? What's "fine"?

Max: Well… We ate well, had a good time here. Now we have to pay appropriately.

Me: Hang on, I don't understand, is this how much you were actually expecting to pay? This *(I stuck my finger in the check)* matches what you intended to pay… and that's supposed to be "appropriate"? Or is that what you call it so that I won't think you are cheap?

Max: I didn't think anything like that, but I say its "appropriate" so it's "appropriate". Not too high, not too low – "appropriate".

Me: And I think *(I flapped the check in front of Max's face)* that it is high, damn it! And that this *(I flapped the check again)* is not appropriate! We did not have this much worth of a good time. Max, before paying, you should check what they scribble on there. *(I began to carefully examine the bill.)* Everybody is so shy, so careful not to display caution and thrift! So coy in front of these gypsies! *(I waved vaguely in the direction of the waiters.)* Meanwhile, they're not shy at all…

Max *(grabbed the check from me):* This is exactly why I should pay, before you start something. Let's not get petty.

Me: What do you mean petty? Quit parading your… provincial hang-ups.

Max: What provincial hang-ups? I just want to pay and that's all! You don't want to pay – don't pay. I am satisfied and feel like paying. I've got money…

Me: I've got money too, so…

Max: Everyone has money. *(Max paused.)* Understand? Everyone! *(Another pause.)* Why are you looking at me like that? Isn't it obvious? Everyone has it. Little old grandmas have some sort of money, kids have it in their piggy banks, even the ones begging on the street… they have money. To some it might not seem like money, but it is. So everybody's got money! And this here, this is money too *(he showed his wallet),* money that I put in here and brought with me just so that I could spend it today. It's like as if this money is already gone. Gone! *(Max opened his wallet and, without taking out the cash, began counting off the amount owed.)*

Me: And why are you covering up your wallet? Huh? Why are you hiding it then?

Max: Why, you want me to wave the money around in front of your face?

Me: Don't wave it around… but don't hide it either. I'm not looking inside your wallet.

Max: Alright already! It's just awkward, that's all…

Me: Yeah right.

Max: "Yeah right" what?

Me: Awkward *(I mocked him).* That's what! It's always like that when it comes to money. Always!

Max: I don't get it! Always what? *(Max handed the money to the waiter and thanked him.)* I don't understand, Sanya, what's this "always"?

Me: You don't get it? Look at you, you're hiding the money from me. Hiding it! Going to the banya with me, to the bathroom… no problem! You tell me all the details about your chicks. Where, with whom, how many times and so forth… About all your sores and pains… You spill everything when I don't even ask. But the money? No, the money – that's too "awkward"! Money is off limits! That's the most hushed subject! Not prohibited, but hushed, right? The most depraved sex acts… hell knows what else… people talk about everything, even though it's seemingly inappropriate, but everyone does anyway! Meanwhile, there isn't anything necessarily taboo in discussing money, but they all avoid discussing it. Even though money is exactly what interests everyone the most. Get it? The most interesting thing isn't who did what with whom and when, but for how much! The most important thing is actually who paid who and how much. For what – that's secondary. The question of "where did you get it?" is less exciting than "how much?" And yet nothing, not a single subject is as hushed as the subject of money. Nothing else hides under the same layer of deception. Everyone lies! Like, for instance, say somebody has a watch, a nice fancy watch. He may've received it as a gift. But in one situation or crowd he'll say that he bought the damn thing in Geneva, and in another he'll lie about buying it for a bottle of vodka from some drunk at a railway station in Smolensk. And then, what do you know – turns out the watch is real gold! And in a third scenario he'll take it off and put it in his pocket so nobody would see it at all. That's right! Waving money around is embarrassing. But driving some expensive fucking car isn't? Wearing half a kilo of gold on your wrist isn't embarrassing? Dolling up your girlfriends… like, I don't know what. Decorating them like Christmas trees so that everyone would say: oh look, she is with him! No problem! But like this? *(I took my wallet, opened it and showed Max how much was inside.)* Never like this! No! "Put your money away", "Don't wave it around", "It's awkward". That's all anybody ever does, wave money around. Fussing over what costs what, instantly judging somebody by what kind of tie or jacket they wear, telling from across the street if it's a brand name or some cheap fake… That's all anybody ever does is flaunt money at each other. They brag a little about their skills, connections, their taste in things, but they always flaunt money in a much bigger way. They just don't do it like this! *(I spread-open my wallet again.)* That would "aaawwwkward!"

Max: Stop it! Here is my money! *(He showed his wallet.)* And I am not embarrassed about it, understand? I didn't find it, nobody gave it to me, I earned it. Don't harass me…

Me: Earned it? Who didn't earn it? Even somebody who, let's say, picks your pocket will also think: "I earned it! Nobody just gave it to me!" Or this gypsy. *(I pointed to the waiter I didn't like.)* You tipped him, didn't you? I'm not asking "how much", I am asking "did you tip him?" Yes, you did! So you see? It may seem like you earned that money... but, in fact, he earned it now!

Max: And I don't mind. Don't mind, I tell you! Let him be three times the gypsy. What do I care? You and I spent time in this warm place, had a conversation, a meal, he stands there smiling to us... so I gave him money. He is happy. I am happy. We're happy. Which means I spent the money well. And that's all there is to it!

Me: Right... but that's not the point... You can't pay so much when there is a...

Max: I already paid. Sanya, enough. Can, can't... whatever. You can't and I can. So stop it. We've been talking about money for too long. It's not worth it, spending so much time on this topic, I don't want to...

Me (shaking my head): "Spending so much time on this topic!" We spend our entire lives on this topic. Our entire lives! We live with money all the time. And as soon as we get our hands on some... that's it! That's how it starts! You give money to kids and right away they know what to with it. Everything else in the world they shove in their mouths, but money – stash it right up and start saving. What for, why – doesn't matter – they just start saving! They don't want to spend their own money – they know that candy and other little things grownups will buy for them. And as soon as they start saving their little cash, they start to cheat. Meanwhile, what could they possibly know about money...? I mean, look – I work. I earn money. I finished school, worked hard, and now I do what I want. Or rather, what I had wanted to do. What I'd always wanted to do, I am now doing. Today, I don't want it as much anymore, but I still do it. After all, that's what I wanted. So I'm doing it. That's my profession, my business, that's me. Understand? Me! So I do it and get paid for doing it. I am not going to work for free. But because I get paid, I generally don't do what I want to do the way I want to do it. Not the way I'd want to do it personally. But that's not what I'm trying to say. Some things are just the way they are... You see, I do the work I'm supposed to do. I don't know how to do anything else, and therefore I cannot want anything else. I love to work! Max, you know this about me. I've done a lot to get here, to work the way I'm working now. That's how I earn a living, my living. But suppose I find some money. Say, lots of money! A fucking million! And it's over! OVER! All the money I have been earning before – the money I am willing to work for – ceases to matter. And just like that, my work turns into some strange hobby. And you know what, I *will* quit work. My whole life, whatever it may be, will be destroyed. Everything will go straight to hell! Everything I'd learned, have been trying to accomplish. My whole life!

I've heard from so many people: "If I had this much money, I'd open SUCH a shop or SUCH a company!" No you wouldn't! And so we don't have SUCH shops… But the scariest thing, Max, is that if I do find that money – I'll still take it! I know that it will destroy my life, but I'll take it anyway. For sure! Because if I merely come into a lot of money, my life is already destroyed. OVER! No matter what! Understand? Even if I don't keep and, like a fool, give it up to the government or find its owner… I'll spend the rest of my life in torment thinking about it. And everyone else will think of me as a fool! The worst type at that: a rotten and disgusting fool.

Max: Sure they will! And they'll hate you too, by the way. They will, no matter what you do. Whether you take the money or not, makes no difference… You know something, Sanya, I like money. The thing itself. Look: for instance, somebody asks me how much my friend is worth, a friend like you let's say. I'll crack a guy right in the eye for even asking me something like this. But when shopping for your birthday present, I go from store to store, thinking: "Alright, this is too cheap for him, and this too expensive". And I choose a gift at a price that's suitable for you. Get it? Meaning, I come up with a specific price! For who? A friend! You! Disgraceful? Yes, but amusing!

Me: No, that's not what I mean. You like money, you don't like money, what's the difference? It exists, and nothing can be done about it. But I wish I didn't feel its presence. Not feel money at all…

Max: What do you mean, not feel it? How?

Me: How? Well, for example, say I buy some strawberries in the winter. Get a craving for strawberries, with milk and sugar, like when we were kids. I can buy it, I have enough money. And yet I'll stop and think that strawberries will taste better in the summer and, most importantly, they'll be cheaper. That's what I don't want to feel. But I also want the first, the very first sweet cherries in June, and to not have to feel like it's too expensive and that in a week they'll be cheaper. Do you understand what I want?

Max: I do. *(Max shrugged his shoulders.)* I would very much want to have a hat that makes me invisible, I want to breathe under water like a fish and have a small private jet, you know, safe and fantastical, the kind that doesn't exist yet. I want all these things! But I don't indulge in this desire. Instead, I think about the money, Sanya. I think about how to come out on the winning end of this little business hustle. I think about whether I should or shouldn't buy a new car, and if I should, what kind. I've got many other, basically similar questions to resolve. But yes, I would like to have the invisible hat, to breath like a fish. And I would really, really like to speak to my father. To speak to him now. At my current age. But my father died... a long time ago. And right before his death, we had a fight... My point is... that it's nice to talk about my father or about a hat that makes you invisible – it's nice and, most of all, not shameful. You know why? Because it's impossible! As for a new car... what the fuck is there to talk about? If I need it – I'll buy one! Sanya, you're not going to be late, are you?

And so ended our chat.

It was as though I was splashed with the world's coldest liquid. I glanced at the watch. The panic settled slightly, I overstayed by only seven-eight minutes. How could I've been so oblivious? To have risked like this? I rushed over to the coat check, Max in tow, spurring me giddily. But I was in no mood for jokes.

"See that, Sanya, the moment you started talking about money, you forgot about love."

The bastard, he was right...

11

It was already ten after seven when I finally got a cab. Whether the car's interior was clean or dirty no longer mattered to me. The most important thing was that it drove. Fast!

"Where exactly? Prospect Mira is long," asked the thin driver with a short haircut.

"I don't remember the building. I'll show you once we're there. It's right on the avenue... I mean, no need to make turns. On the right side..." nervous, I struggled to formulate thoughts.

"Alright, got it," the driver said. "Are we in a rush?"

"We are late," I quickly answered.

"Well, in that case, let's try..." he sang the usual driver song.

"Of course, of course! Obviously! If we get there in forty minutes," I interrupted his pitch, "I'll make it worth your while."

There was a dreadful number of cars on the road. I could be late easily. Already past seven! Hardly a joke. Moscow was nearly at a standstill. But my driver...

He had this amazing way of driving. Very lanky and tall, he didn't sit back in the seat – instead he was hunched over the steering wheel as if in an attempt to push his nose right up against the windshield. He was constantly moving his long arms and legs – pressing pedals, switching gears and steering continuously. He was twirling his pointy head in search of every possible opening. As soon as he found one – he'd make an instant run for it. And while doing all this, he never stopped commenting on the actions of other drivers. As he passed somebody, he would look over his shoulder and say: "Oh, sure. Glasses! Jackass! Can't see in front of..." or "Of course! A skirt! I knew it!" or "Where do they buy their driver's licenses?" and so on. To him, being out on the street was like being at war. It was as though he was pushing forward in short dashes, constantly analyzing the changing conditions of battle and making instant strategic decisions.

His car was also almost like a military vehicle. It lacked anything superfluous. In place of the radio was a gaping black hole with wires sticking out of the darkness. The driver caught my gaze.

"It got stolen a month ago now. Stepped away to take a piss, came back – gone. Never thought anybody would get a hard-on for this radio. Guess I was wrong. They'll steal anything!" He talked quickly, as though firing short bursts. "This car is already fifteen years old. And they still tried to jack it three times just this year. Except no one can start it but me. So it's pointless," he said, sticking a cigarette in his mouth and lighting up.

"Excuse me," I said right way. "Do you mind not smoking, I have asthma," I lied. I didn't want him to smoke. It didn't bother me at all, but I didn't want to stink of smoke when I met Her. I lied about asthma not to offend the driver.

"Sorry," he said and flicked the cigarette nimbly out of the slightly opened window. He would sharply jerk his wobbly car, its every part rattling loudly, and just as sharply hit the brakes. Out of habit, I too was pressing my foot against a nonexistent brake.

"Don't brake," he noticed my movements, "don't be scared. I used to drive an ambulance. We'll make it, don't piss your pants!"

He kept talking the whole time. And I realized that I was so afraid to be late. And yet what was there to be afraid of? If I looked at the situation differently... How late could I really be, ten minutes? Why wouldn't she understand? Of course she would. So we'll have twenty minutes together instead of thirty. So what? To say to Her what I wanted to say, a minute would be enough. And if I don't resolve to tell Her that I love Her today... love the way I've never loved before... Then what good are even two hours, or three... But for whatever reason, it became clear that I must not be late. Better to arrive five-ten minutes earlier... I wanted to catch my breath before we met.

We moved very slowly. The driver was a sprightly one, but he couldn't do the impossible. I shrank into a ball and stared at a single point. No alternate reading of the situation in the vein of, it's alright to be a little late, no big deal, was helping at all. Had I known that there was one chance in a million that I could be late, I would not have gone to the restaurant with Max and would instead have gone to see Her directly. I'd sit there and wait for her, untroubled.

I stared at a single point with a blind, unfocused gaze, heard and didn't hear the driver's rambling next to me, the noise of the street outside, the beating of my heart within…

I actually physically felt how this enormous city was robbing, sucking out of me my time; how Moscow, with the full extent its force, was multiplying my despair…

To avoid constantly checking my watch, I closed my eyes and…

I saw springtime…

I wasn't escorted, I couldn't be. I stood at the platform in front of my train car. It was one of the first spring days. Very bright sun, very tall sky and extremely discernable odors of early thaw. A small brass band played next to the building of the railway station. There was a large crowd of people. Military men, officers and lower ranks had already changed out of their crude winter uniforms. Everyone was elegant, steam-pressed, decked out in stars and medals. The women were all dressed up, their hair styled, wearing light colors.

They were all couples next to my car. Except me. I was alone. This was the car for the departing officers, released from hospitals after their wounds. They stood with their ladies and wives. Some were silent, others chatted unstoppably, but all looked each other in the eyes and held hands.

Our train was to travel far. Epaulettes and patches, as well as peaked caps, peak-less caps and forage hats of every military order flashed everywhere. New recruits were taken to the tail end of the train. Already herded aboard, they stuck their heads out of every window to bid farewell to their kin. Mostly older women crowded there, they pressed themselves to windows, saying things in a hurry, afraid to run out time to say everything. Tears ran like streams next to those last few cars. Next to ours – they merely dripped. But these were the tears of real parting. Here, those who said their goodbyes knew, or at least surmised, that they would never see each other again, no matter what happened.

Despite it being a gross violation of the uniform code, as I approached the station I completely unbuttoned the coat and two top buttons of the tunic. I also removed the cap and carried it by the peak. All my things fit inside a small briefcase… Near the train station, I bought some fresh newspapers and… a small bouquet of tulips. Five tulips.

I know nothing about flowers, but I like tulips. Especially the very first, small ones, with tightly closed buds. Tulips squeak when they touch each other inside the bouquet. They are juicy and it make you want to eat them… or at least bite off a small piece of the stem.

I bought them for no reason… just felt like buying something. Out there, where our train was headed, there would be no need for money. I knew that nobody was coming to say goodbye to me. The flowers were bought… for no reason at all.

I shouldn't have bought those tulips. The moment flowers appeared in my hands, a whole heap of sensations having to do with holding flowers crashed down upon me. I reached my train car, stepped inside, looked around my compartment, sat briefly in my seat, placed the briefcase on the shelf and even removed my coat, but I couldn't stay there and read the paper. I picked up the tulips and went back out to the platform.

I caught myself carefully watching the faces of all the women around me. I was searching the crowd with my eyes, searching for Her face. But it was clear. She couldn't have possibly been here, in this small town. She couldn't know that I was standing at this platform and that my train was about to depart. "She can't be here!" I kept telling myself. But there were flowers in my hand, so I must have been looking for Her in the crowd.

Then I suddenly realized that I kept glancing at the station clock… and my own watch. I realized that I *was* waiting for Her. Waiting as though she was certain to come. I realized that it was impossible. But there were tulips in my hand, so I kept waiting.

Then I heard a toot. Strange, since there were so many loud sounds around the station, including toots. But this toot was recognized and acknowledged by everybody. Couples began to part, somebody stood at the window writing something across the glass with a finger, somebody was speaking soundlessly on the other side of the window. Couples parted. At the tail end of the train, women began to wail. As though having taken more air into its lungs, the small brass orchestra began playing, louder than usual, a march, so masterfully played and impossibly melancholy.

I stood still and was the last of the departing to remain at the platform. There were calls for me to board the train at once.

All the sounds in my ears quieted, the movement of people around me slowed. I raised my eyes to the station clock, then higher... up to the sky. At that moment, the train cars clanged. The train lurched and moved from a standstill. In three steps, I caught up to the open door, got up on the step and felt the movement of the train. I turned back, looked with a slow, long gaze over the lingering platform, and for whatever reason slowly raised my left hand again to check my watch. A second later I tossed the flowers into the gap between the platform and the moving train. Now free of the flowers, my hand slipped into the inside pocket. From there, I pulled out a small blue silk handkerchief – Her only gift to me. I brought the handkerchief to my face and inhaled a faint scent of perfume.

Another three seconds, and sounds, colors and the rush of life returned...

Shrunk into a ball, I sat on the front seat of an old car, clamped up in Moscow traffic. The driver next to me was moving all his limbs. With my left hand, I was touching the smooth neckerchief tied around my neck.

I started to smile, because I suddenly realized that I was treating this neckerchief as if it were Her gift... As if She were the one who gave it to me... and this scent were Hers...

"Come on, let's go already! Move..." my driver was saying to somebody. I glanced at the watch. Of my forty minute bonus time only eight minutes were remaining, and we were barely at the turn to the Avenue of Peace. The traffic jam was simply inhuman!

"Where did they all come from?" The driver wouldn't quit.

We were late and I was about to call Her and warn that I wasn't going to be on time. We made a turn onto the avenue, which was also jammed.

"And here's our locomotive!" My companion announced with joy. I didn't understand what he meant. But at that very second, an ambulance passed us from the left, flashing and wailing. Abruptly, he jerked the car to the right, lined up behind the ambulance and rushed after it. His gusto dealt a brilliant blow to civility and traffic, to prudence and good road manners. We flew ahead. "This ambulance was sent to me," I thought.

"We'll make it," the driver laughed. "I want to get rid of you already. I need a smoke so bad, it's not even funny!"

EVGENY GRISHKOVETS

I looked at him. We are probably the same age. I wonder, which one of us is older?

"What're you looking at? You look pretty strong for an asthmatic! I don't suffer from that myself, knock on wood. Only my back, it gets me sometimes…"

We made it in forty-two minutes, but I paid him twice what I owed.

12

We had met once before in this café. It was a small and unremarkable café with six tables. Grey floor, beige walls, a bar, round little tables, photos of old trains and airplanes on the walls... Nothing spectacular or special... But we had already met there once... so this place was more important and dearer to me than the trendiest and best designed establishments.

There was only one table available, right by the door. The rest were all taken and the people were in no hurry to leave. I sat down at that table, took off my coat, scarf, placed them on the next chair and checked the watch. It was seven to eight. I sat with my back to the entrance so that I wouldn't see the street or the door. Knowing myself, if I could see the street – I'd be looking in that direction and the waiting would become even tougher.

She was supposed to enter from the right. There, at the edge of the building which stood on the other side of the Avenue, was the entrance to her office – a blue glowing sign, the name of the firm, and also a glowing little plane and little ship. Very charming. I very much wanted to walk in there and see Her at Her workplace, but did not dare do that.

I sat in a manner that wouldn't allow me to see the door from which she was to appear. Since childhood, whenever I really looked forward to something and looked in that direction, whatever it was, I never had enough patience to wait for it, either that or I would miss the moment it arrived. For instance, my mom and I would come to the train station to meet my father, and as I waited I looked toward the place where the rails, on which my father's train was to arrive, curved around the bend. I very much wanted to see the train's arrival. But the train was running late. Three minutes, five, six... So I would get distracted for a few seconds... To ask my mother something or buy something she asked me... And when I turned back, the train was already in view... The magical moment of appearance was missed... That's how it always happened, with everything. So I figured that it was I who delayed the expected by looking. So I turned my back to the door.

This past month, the number of people calling me – and therefore the number of calls in general – has greatly decreased. I simply stopped expressing joy about every call. I instantly declined invitations to various events and tried not to engage in any negotiations. Gradually, the calls became less and less frequent. I was just as glad about this as I was, four years ago, about nonstop calls from clients, colleagues, friends and women... I felt successful, felt needed, that people wanted me around not just as someone who performed certain types of work, but as an interlocutor, a companion... Back then, in Moscow, my social circle suddenly increased, new routes, addresses, new faces appeared...

A month ago, I concluded that it was all a sham and nonsense. I had built one decent house and that was it. That house has remained my sole calling card, but it was still enough for Moscow.

There was more silence now. Even calls like these quieted: "Where have you been hiding?" or "Are you scheming something or what? You don't call, you don't write!" or "Babe, you're not sick, are you? Everyone's lost touch with you!" I grumbled back something unhappy to all these calls. Hers was the only call I awaited. She has never called me once. No, it's not that there has ever been a time when she promised to call and didn't. It's that I was always the one to call.

But to call just because, in the middle of the day, or night, or in the morning, just to hear my voice, that she has never done. That's not how She is! I was thrilled by that... But if She ever called, at least once – that would bring me sheer happiness. I have waited for that call... Her call... Always.

I have been happy about things at work lately. A year ago, we were working on six construction, restoration and reconstruction projects at the same time. Me, Grisha (my assistant), and our secretary and bookkeeper could hardly keep up with all the documents, agreements and other stuff. The sites were uninteresting, I was stressed out, straining myself, and realized that I couldn't handle it... It was a terrible blow to my ego...

But now we were contracted for only two sites. I decided not to take any new ones until we finish them. Besides, it was time to quit fiddling with these shops and pharmacies. In Moscow, you can keep doing them until the end of time. That and requests started to come in from the dear and no so dear deep provinces. After all, I was now a full blown Moscow architect!

For all my dislike of Moscow, there was something about this city that spread evenly all over the motherland. Moscowness – it was the best trademark.

I still remember with perfect clarity the billboard on the wall of the city philharmonic back in my hometown. The billboard announced a concert of the local symphony orchestra. All the information about the orchestra, the names of great composers whose compositions our orchestra were to perform – it was all printed in blue type of small to medium size. The word "conductor" was also punched in blue. Only "David Tsitsilyan. Moscow" was ablaze in large red letters.

I didn't respond to any offers from outside the Capital's limits. I was yet to learn how to exploit this magic word "Moscow", which for some reason is always associated with the color red... Alright, fine! I won't lie. I've gotten used to it. I didn't want to leave Moscow. I had everything here. And now there was Her. As for business, I had distanced myself from it... and was happy about that.

She, by the way, also moved to Moscow about ten years ago. She came from somewhere far. She told me about it. A city much farther away than where I came from. She was too good for me...

I sat and waited. My entire torso froze and stopped communicating cues about its boundaries and depths. Only the head and the heart were functioning. At exactly eight I began to slip rapidly into despair. At 8:07, I called Her.........

The strange thing was, I somehow knew She wouldn't come. Knew it right away, even before we agreed to make a date...

I didn't get upset. I couldn't be upset at Her. I couldn't even think of or imagine a situation in which I could get upset at Her. And I wasn't disappointed. No! It was as though I fell out of an airplane at top altitude and speed. In other words, I was freezing and suffocating at the same time...

She didn't answer right away. I had to wait nine or ten rings... In fact, though She was late by only seven minutes, I somehow sensed that she wouldn't show up at all...

Her voice was very distant. She told me in all sincerity, that only when I called did she check the time and was mortified when she did. She asked for my forgiveness. She was forced to deal with some problems and had to leave the office. She was unable to warn me...

EVGENY GRISHKOVETS

She also said that she couldn't call, though she remembered that it was something she was supposed to do.

I asked if something happened with her daughter... She said no... And that she couldn't talk anymore, said we should talk tomorrow, said one more time that she was sorry and hung up.

"So," I thought.

"So," I said out-loud and repeated it indefinitely.

"I need help!" I thought. "Somebody help me!" Then I got a sharp sense that I all had the whole day was four cups of coffee and a bottle of kefir and haven't once... gone to the bathroom. My body sent me a distress signal...

I got up and went to the bathroom. There I urinated, cried a little, washed up, stood awhile holding on to the sink and looking into my eyes in the mirror. It was at that moment that I broadcast a tremendously powerful message of suffering and despair. If satellites in space picked up this message, then several of them would spin out of their orbits. Then I left the bathroom.

"Could you not leave your phone like that please?" I heard a voice, turned around and saw the bartender. A dark-haired, obviously southern man in a white shirt, black vest and nice glasses. "Not a good idea leaving it by the door. I am watching of course, but... Are you alright?"

After two minutes, I was sitting on a high stool at the bar, drinking cola with ice and dialing Max's number.

"You nearly turned green... I thought, this man is about collapse," said the dark-haired barman. He had a tag on his chest. There was one word on it – Eric. Eric was at least fifty years old.

I realized that I was in urgent need of Max. Let him come here and take me away. Take me somewhere, pour me some vodka, force me to eat something. Let him scold me for losing it, or simply chat with me on any topic. I couldn't be alone.

"But this isn't the limit. I haven't hit bottom yet...! No! This isn't the bottom. There is still plenty of room to fall," I thought.

It was so good there! In the dessert, down in the trench by the machine gun, in the cold dark sea... very good! In the train car of the army echelon... it was calm. Cold and calm. There was salvation there, because there wasn't any hope. None! Not even a shadow of hope!

Also, it would be nice to be located at some polar station. To have a little cabin amid the endless ice and snow. Cold ocean separated the snow and ice from continents where it was warm, where there was life. It would be nice to live at such a station for many months, if not years. To have with me a glum and taciturn companion with whom I would exchange two-three words a day. As in: me: "Tea?" Him: "Fine." Four hours later: him: "Get some firewood?" Me: "Fine." In the evening: me: "Who is going to check the equipment tonight?" Him: "Me." And that's all. Enough said. For our cabin to be small, but cozy, warm, but not hot. The little window would always be frosted – either glowing bright with the polar sun, or darkened by the polar night. I would have to establish daily contact, to report something somewhere… (What else do polar explorers do?) It would also be necessary to carefully keep a special journal. To leave the cabin three times a day to check the readings on some type of equipment (meaning, if I were an actually polar explorer, I would know how to do it and know why it was important). If I had a partner, we would obviously take turns: take turns taking the readings, making journal entries, cleaning, cooking, establishing contact with "the mainland". The food would be very monotonous and plain. But I would have no problem with that at all. It would be necessary to have many books. Thick and endless old novels. To reread everything or read anew! There would have to be all of Jules Verne, Walter Scott, Stevenson, Mark Twain, no Dostoevsky or Tolstoy! Dickens? Allowed! "The Captain's Daughter" and "The Belkin Tales", also nice to have, though, sadly Pushkin wrote only a few such gems. In all, nothing contemporary and not too much of the home-grown. "Uncork a bottle of champagne and reread The Marriage of Figaro" – that would be wonderful… I suppose. I cannot do that. I cannot! For the simple reason that I did not read "The Marriage of Figaro". So how could I possibly reread it? And how could there be champagne at a polar station…? Also, every three months a plane would fly by, not land, but fly over us, tip its wings in greeting, drop crates with equipment, provisions, presents, books. But no letters. None!

Also, it would be nice to be in prison. Not in a Russian prison, not today and not for a crime. But just because… for reasons not exactly clear and in a French prison… From a long time ago. Not even a prison, but a fortress. Stone walls, wooden door with metal rivets, fresh hay on the floor, a high-up window with bars and a blue sky.

EVGENY GRISHKOVETS

There would have to be only one book – a heavy ancient Bible, and nothing else. One should, finally, read the whole Bible! I would always have clean, fresh shirts with loose sleeves and narrow cuffs. Not the shirts we have today, thin ones, but the kind made of thick canvas. I would always be clean shaven (By the way, I wonder how they shaved over there, back then… a long time ago). It would be nice to have a barber come in and shave me every morning… And, occasionally, to have a priest come in and have conversations with me. We would have philosophical discussions, endless and laid-back… I could play chess with the guard. They would bring me good bread, apples and a pitcher of wine. As long as there is no chance to pass a note to somebody or receive a letter. And to know for sure that there is no possibility of escape, to know that no one has ever escaped or even attempted to. To have peace of mind, no unavenged grievances or debts of honor. To be certain that I've been put there forever! And that there is absolutely no sense in waiting for a change in power and pardon. None! And so be it, to the very end!

It would be great to be a monk, but not an Orthodox one, with a long and unruly beard. I don't want to live in a cold cell, to live on watery soup and sour cabbage, eating at a communal table with men like myself (if I were a monk), bearded, pale, stooped and unattractive people. I don't want to do crude and wretched work, mostly in the winter and out in the cold. No! I'd like to be a monk somewhere far-far away, where there are beautiful landscapes, quiet, and carp is swimming in a little lake. Where it's beautiful, with mountains and plains, not too hot or too cold. Where I can finally shave my head once and for all. There wouldn't be a single book. Everything is already known to everyone there. I would exhaust my body with the most complicated exercises, learn tranquility and strength, greet sunrise and part with the sun at dusk while sitting in the same pose. A man of true wisdom and authority would come into my life there – my mentor. An undoubtedly small, skinny man, seeing right through me and always three steps ahead. He would teach me to hear rain and distinguish the song of the cricket from the trill of the cicada, teach me to see the clouds and understand them, to walk through the fog and always end up by the temple. There, I would write my first poem… with a twig in the sand. A poem about rain, clouds, crickets, cicada… about fog and sand. But not a word about myself. Not one word!

I would also agree to go on a permanent space mission. A mission that would not return, and if it did, it would be when there is no one left on earth who could be waiting for me. Time doesn't pass the same way in space as it does on earth. I would fly away knowing that I would never see or hear Her again. I would be put to sleep to wake up hundreds of years from now, millions of parsecs away from earth. I would wake in a world in which She doesn't exist! But if She were the one to fly away… I wouldn't be able to stay. No! EVERYTHING here would remind me of Her, and I wouldn't be able to not wait for Her… I couldn't possibly stay here…

Max answered his phone. Thank God!

"Max, get over here right away!"

"Sanya, how about you come here, there's a…"

"Fuck, Max! I'm begging you! Come down here, please! Take me away from here!"

"What happened?" Max asked more seriously now.

"Max! Come. Please."

"Sanya… where are you?"

"The Avenue of Peace. If you go toward downtown…" I realized that I wouldn't be able to coherently explain the directions, "Max, I'm giving the phone to someone who'll explain everything. Please, just hurry!"

I passed the phone to Eric and asked him to break down the route to my friend. Eric picked up my phone and took his time explaining to Max, patiently, thoroughly, even gesturing, how to get there.

"He'll be here soon," Eric said, returning my phone. "Are you sure you're alright? Some tea maybe? Or… something stronger?"

"No, no. Everything is fine. Did my friend say where he was coming from?"

"He asked how to get here from New Arbat."

"Oh, that's far…" I figured I'd have to sit here and wait at least forty minutes. That's terrible! But to go somewhere on my own? No way! I'll wait.

I really wanted a drink, and to drink it in a single gulp.

13

"Are you sure you wouldn't like anything?" asked the barman, squinting suspiciously. "More cola perhaps?"

"Yes, please."

"Lots of ice?"

"Lots of ice."

"With lemon, but no straw?"

"Exactly!" For a half-second I was surprised that Eric the bartender knew how I liked my cola, when I saw in front of me a glass with the remains of cola, ice and a circle of lemon. I must've already ordered it like that. I just couldn't remember.

Eric worked quiet skillfully. There weren't that many tables, but a young stocky waitress constantly approached him with orders. He did everything swiftly, yet his hands moved smoothly and somehow separately from his calm face. He clearly enjoyed conversation. And he spoke with a southern tenderness and insinuation.

"By the way, please excuse me, but you are not by any chance a writer, are you?" He asked, smiling.

"No, definitely not a writer," I answered.

"And...?"

"And not a poet or artist, not even a journalist."

"Please, excuse me..." he expressed embarrassment, but continued nonetheless. He really wanted to tell me a story.

Here is what Eric the bartender told me.

"I just thought you might be a writer... There was a time when I also despaired. Very much so. About five years ago. Back then I was still working at the Hotel Ukraine... Wait, no! Not five, eight years ago! You see that? That's life, I'm starting to forget things... So anyway, I was then working at the Hotel Ukraine upstairs, at the bar. It was one of those nasty autumns, there was love in my life, or maybe there wasn't, this and that. So basically, I also fell into a malaise, a worry. My mood was so bad that I could cry. All I wanted was to buy myself a neckerchief. I went to a store – this one, that one, went to the market. Couldn't find one that I liked. I didn't really want to buy one that was for women. All those generic, synthetic ones - didn't seem right either. I never wore such scarves, wouldn't even know where they were sold. Then somebody told me. I went to that store. They had really nice neckerchiefs. Different ones! I thought: 'I'll buy three!' I ask the young woman: 'My dear, how much is that one?' You wouldn't believe what she said! I took my head in my hands, like this *(Eric showed me how he grabbed his head)*, and I tell her: 'This tiny thing here? It costs that much?' I started to feel awkward in front of this young lady, that I couldn't afford to buy this little neckerchief. Imagine how much a suit must cost in that store? I turned red. Counted the money. It was barely enough for that neckerchief, the plainest one. I took the metro on the way back.

"I started wearing that neckerchief with a shirt. Very nice, everybody liked it. I could tell, too – it looked good. And once I noticed that one of the patrons was also wearing one around his neck. Some tall foreigner. A bit older than me. He was there as a representative of some big corporation… from Holland. A pleasant fellow, polite. He'd order two-three beers each evening and sit there, reading. He started talking to me. He spoke Russian well. Very impressive! He'd stay longer than everybody else. And one time, he sat not at the table, but at the bar. Sad looking, writing something, not talking to me. And then, right before leaving, as if by accident, he dropped a note for me on the counter. I took the note, in it was a message for me, beautiful handwriting. Sure, it had some mistakes in it. But it's not like I can write in his language, so good for him – he wrote it in Russian! He wrote that he invited me, if I had some free time, to have dinner together. And that was that!

"After that, I never wear a neckerchief."

That was the story Eric the bartender told me.

"Sorry, but I won't be inviting you for dinner. My friend is on his way," I said.

Eric laughed for a good couple of minutes. He liked my joke very much. Except I wasn't joking, at that moment I was incapable of joking. I was tormented, tortured, torn to pieces by a single question:

EVGENY GRISHKOVETS

what happened to Her, what is going on and, more than anything else, why didn't She turn to me for help? Who else could she turn to but me? Couldn't she tell that I was in love with Her? Of course she could! Why wouldn't she permit me the joy of helping Her? My God! If only she let me help Her! Why doesn't She trust me?!

My phone rang. I shuddered, everything inside me turned upside down and something broke off and fell all the way down to my heels. A freight train got derailed somewhere in South Africa…

It wasn't Her calling. I heard an unfamiliar voice. A young woman's voice.

"Good evening, is this Alexander? I'm sorry to bother you."

"Yes, it's alright."

"Hello again, this is Marina. I mean, my name is Marina. I am Grisha's wife."

"Excuse me, what Grisha?"

"What do you mean? Grisha! The one who works with you…"

"Oh, Grisha! Of course! Did something happen?"

"No, no. Nothing happened, no need to worry… Please forgive me for calling you," her voice sounded very young.

"How old is she?" I thought. Grisha is twenty-five. I didn't even know he was married. He never talked about himself. I hired him two years ago, but I didn't know anything about his life.

"Grisha doesn't know that I'm calling you. He won't be happy if he finds out."

"If I understand you correctly, you don't want me to tell Grisha that you called? Right?"

"Yes… But…" already anxious, she now sounded completely discomforted. "Can you talk now? Do you have two minutes? I am not interrupting, am I?"

"I do have two minutes," I said too severely. She, on the other hand, spoke politely, nervously, in a dignified manner. Besides, it was clear that something has happened, something serious. Otherwise, she wouldn't be calling. "Don't worry, please go ahead. You're not really interrupting."

"Thank you! I got your phone number from Grisha's phone book… Not sure where to begin… Grisha respects you very much. Always speaks of you with admiration… That you're such a professional and a nice man… You are such an example for him… He simply loves you…

He is really worried about all that's been happening… He usually tells me very little about business, about work, but he is always happy to talk about you. He is proud…"

"Thank you! You're embarrassing me. So what's really the…" I began, but she cut me off.

"Yes, of course! I'm sorry. You see, lately, especially the last few days, he is just not himself. Doesn't eat anything, barely sleeps. Yesterday, he cried in the bathroom. He tells me nothing. And today, an hour ago, he came home, I set the table, he sat down, sat there in silence, didn't touch anything. Then he said that he failed you terribly, that he is worthless, that he doesn't understand why you even tolerate him… Then he said that today you resolved a problem that he couldn't handle by himself… That he had spent a week trying to tackle it, but couldn't and ruined everything instead. And you showed up, took one look around and fixed everything in five minutes. He also said that you didn't really need him, that he only gets in your way and you only tolerate him out of pity. Then he got dressed and left the house. And you know, Alexander, he cried again. Please understand, he really appreciates you and tries very hard. And if he falls short, it's not on purpose or out of laziness or neglect. He is very decent, believe me, I'm so worried. Where did he go?"

I heard the young woman start to cry.

"Marina! Marinochka! Don't worry. I really value Grisha. He is an excellent specialist, a responsible worker and a wonderful friend. I couldn't run things without him. I respect him very much. You should be proud of him. Tell me, he left the house… Did he take his phone with him?"

"I don't know," she said, sobbing, "let me check." I heard footsteps and other sounds. She was looking for the phone. "Can't find it. I'll call him and check."

"Don't even think about calling him now! I'll call him myself. And then I'll call you. I'll call you regardless. Please wait a little bit and do not worry. Thank you for calling me." I hung up.

"My God," I thought. "How infantile!"

I instantly recalled a totally desperate look in Grisha's eyes, his stooped, almost hunched pose, his attempts at saying something… This is what it turns out to be! Turns out this is how awful he is feeling! And for what? For who? Because I fell in love, because of me? Poor Grisha!

He hasn't realized that what he and I are doing – it's bullshit. That guys like us… we're dime a dozen. Sure, we're not the worst, but there are better ones, a lot better. How many thousands of crews are there in this city alone, large and small, building, renovating, rebuilding. And how many architects like me – a shitload! Exactly like me: fussy, selfish, ambitions, unkind… How was I different?

Meanwhile, the poor guy thought that he was doing something important, afraid to let me down, to not live up to my confidence, my trust. There was nothing more important to him. Poor thing! Poor, poor thing!

I quickly found and dialed his number… "Please answer!" I couldn't carry this load on top of everything else. I had to resolve this right away.

I remember how back in school, sitting in the cafeteria, I thought… I was about thirteen-fourteen. I thought, looking at the lunch ladies working in the kitchen… I began calculating roughly how many schools there were in our city. Probably, no less than eighty. Each school has a lunch room and there is a minimum of four cooks working in the kitchen. And how many other workplaces do we have, various factories, plants, how many large offices, hospitals, transportation hubs and so on and on. And they all have cafeterias, buffets, different types of small cafes. And they all employ people who spend their entire lives cooking bad food. They're bad cooks! And yet there was a time when they were children, like me, (as I said, I was then thirteen-fourteen). And they didn't think that they'd become cooks. They had first names, last names… they were individual people. Unique! And yet they work as bad cooks. Then who are they? They are – BAD COOKS! That's all they are. Nothing else! What does that say about life?

I remember being proud of my last name. To me, it seemed rare and refined. I assumed that I had a rare destiny! Whenever I played football in the courtyard, I always imagined that, for sure, some football trainer would pass by. He would look at me and how I play, and think: "Here is an excellent young man, a real talent…" And then he'd ask one of the other boys: "Who is that kid? That one, in a blue t-shirt?" I figured that my last name would be mentioned. I couldn't possibly fade away, like those people who became cooks… Not me!

And I continued to imagine that I did not fade away. I work in Moscow. In Moscow! What can be farther away? It is the limit! I work here! I am the man! I put my name on my blueprints… But so what? I have built one decent house, on one of the small streets of one of Moscow's many suburban towns. And that's it! Otherwise, I mostly grind and grind, like a bark beetle, carving new tributaries into the endless labyrinth of Moscow. There are more guys like me in Moscow than cooks in my hometown! I hope Grisha answers……...

He did.

"Hello," Grisha answered in a calm, polite voice.

"Grisha! Good thing I reached you. It's me, Alexander, your boss." I tried speaking in a happy, unforced tone. "So? How are you, how's the mood?"

"Everything's fine. I left the site at seven. The guys are almost finished with the garbage. Everyone is in a good mood. Starting tomorrow, we'll be replacing…"

"The hell with the site! Grigoriy, I noticed that you were quite overworked…"

"No, no! I am not overworked at all. I am sorry, but I am not at all…" he cut me off.

I shouldn't have mentioned anything about being overworked, shouldn't have said that to him.

"No, Grisha, please, that's not what I meant to say! I didn't feel right about our meeting today…"

"It's totally my fault. I just didn't know how to tell you…"

"Grisha! Please, let me finish! If there is somebody's fault here, it's not yours. I am the one who has neglected things lately. I am the one who's been slacking off! You know, if it weren't for you, Grisha, everything would collapse by now. I am really glad that you work with me. I trust you completely and, if you'll forgive me for saying so, abuse your sense of responsibility and decency. I've been meaning to tell you this earlier, but it wouldn't be right in front of the workers, and other times somehow didn't work out. We should get together after work! What do you think? Are you married, Grisha?"

"Yes… my wife, Masha… I mean, Marina!"

"There you go! Wonderful! Let's hang out sometime, go to the movies. I'll bring a friend too… this woman. We'll go to the movies, then get dinner. How does that sound to you, Grisha?"

"I don't know, I'll ask Marina."

EVGENY GRISHKOVETS

"Nonsense, Grisha! Don't be shy. We'll figure something out tomorrow. Introduce me to your wife. O.K.?!"

"Alright," Grisha said in bewilderment, but in a good way. The right kind of bewildered. "Thank you!"

"Thank me later. Let's touch base tomorrow and figure it out. Keep up the good work. Send my best to your wife. And don't worry. Everything is fine, you're a good man! Later!" I almost said: "Go home!"

"Good bye. Thank you so much! I'll tell Marina," he actually laughed. "Good bye!"

How wonderful to see and hear people who are happy! How easy it is sometimes to bring them joy, if only for a short time. "Let me make another person happy," I thought and called Grisha's wife.........

She was delighted and thanked me endlessly until I had to hang up.

But only one call, only one voice in the world could save me. But She wasn't going to call, I knew that much.

14

While Eric was telling me his story about the neck scarf, while I talked to Grisha's wife and Grisha himself, the café completely filled up. That's Moscow for you! Even the most uninteresting café, with the dullest interior and selection of drinks and food, is still packed on a Friday night. It was becoming smoky and noisy. Eric was saying something to me periodically, I didn't listen, only nodded and smiled in response whenever I knew that he was finished telling another joke or punctuated another thought. Max was supposed to arrive any minute.

I heard the door open behind me for the umpteenth time. I turned around – another joyful young couple had come in. It must have started to snow. The man and the woman had small snow mounds on their shoulders. Joyously and loudly they dusted themselves off, stomped their feet, shaking the snow from their shoes, and just as joyously went back outside. I saw all this in my peripheral vision. My attention was caught by a fairly large man, who sat at the same table I was sitting at before. Tall, broad-shouldered, hair with noticeable gray, combed up and to the back. A dark-grey turtleneck sweater. A nice, expressive face. Groomed. His face seemed familiar to me, very much in fact, but I couldn't place it. He sat with a cup of coffee, a mineral water and an ashtray. He was staring at the table, thinking about something intensely. I didn't look at him directly, careful not to attract his attention.

I remember, when I first moved to Moscow, I saw somebody I knew at a restaurant… Already slightly drunk, I was delighted, came up to him, slapped him on the shoulder, said "Hello…" He stared back totally perplexed. I said to him "What do you mean? It's me…!" Turned out, he was a TV news anchor from Channel Two. I simply wasn't used to the fact that you could meet people from TV in real life. Back in my hometown, if you saw someone you thought you knew – you knew them. But this was Moscow. One had to be more delicate.

The man's face was familiar. A thoroughbred face. It was quite possible that he was an actor or a writer...

I turned away... Meaning, turned back to the bar, slightly puzzled. I needed a drink and soon. "Max! Where are you, Max!?" I spoke soundlessly, like a spell.

I sharply turned my head sideways, then turned it back, and because of that saw the bar counter sway and move somewhere off to the side. I had to get something to eat.

I looked at my hands, they rested on the bar. Not very large hands, nails clipped neatly... Just hands. My hands. I bought gloves for them about a month ago, now I have to buy new ones. Out of love, out of exhaustion and absentmindedness, because my neck was itchy and irritated, out of joy of acquiring a blue neckerchief, I left my gloves in the taxi. I've deserted my hands. Now they lay powerless in front of me. There wasn't much strength left in them. "I don't take good care of my body," I thought. Soon Max will come, we'll start drinking, the hands will pour and bring shot glasses or tumblers up to my mouth. And both my hands and I... we realize that it would only get worse later. That the best thing would be to go home, take a shower, go to sleep and get some rest. And in the morning, to have breakfast and... do something useful for myself. But no. The hands will not resist... They will pour...

My body brought me so much joy when I was little. It was as if it didn't exist at all. I never thought about what I should or shouldn't eat, meaning how it would affect my health or figure. My body could run, jump without tiring, swim in the river till it turned blue without freezing, fall asleep in any position. And when I slept, you could carry my body around, put it anywhere, dress and undress it – I wouldn't wake up. It thrilled me constantly that it could easily learn to ride a bicycle, ice skate... And that it grew! It grew out of shoes, out of pants and jackets. I used to be proud of it. I used to love it. And now all I do is torment it.

My hands... and the rest of my body might ask me: "Why are you torturing us? What have we done wrong? We don't ask much of you. We require decent food, regular sleep, occasional fresh air. Some kind of exercise wouldn't be so bad, at least walking. You should walk sometimes! Not to get somewhere in a rush, but walk... just to walk. After all, we, your organs, do everything, we try, we produce hair, nails, sweat, saliva and other life-sustaining juices. We work too hard! And we are tired of you! We don't understand, can't figure out which organ is responsible for what anymore, or what's going on with you. The heart? Oh, no. It's not all that happy any more either. Sure, it's still strong, knock on wood… Still, you have to explain this… What happened? What really happened?"

Really, what did happen? She couldn't make it? Then I suppose she couldn't. She'll explain everything later. It's not like she was doing it to spite me. No. She is always so caring. Can't she sense how much I love her? Of course she can. A woman like that! Of course she can sense it. She knows it for sure!

"What if She loves me too?" This simple thought struck me. I was stunned by that thought. Until that moment, I thought that it wasn't important for me whether she loved me or not, that my own love did not depend on that. And then, all of a sudden, I understood that perhaps it was hard on her right now too. That, maybe, she has been living these last weeks in her own unbearable condition, and there I was… an egotist! Egotist!!! A fucking fool! "Of course She loves me! Maybe She is feeling worse than me. And it's certainly more difficult for her. And here I am…"

Suddenly, this thought made me want to jump up and rush out somewhere… but where? To Her, of course!!! But where? From this thought, everything inside started to tremble… but I felt better. Much better! I am such a bastard. I imagined that she wasn't well, maybe even worse off than I was… And that made me happy…

Somebody's hand lay on my shoulder. Somebody put a hand on my shoulder. Somebody interrupted my dialogue with my own body and the succession of revolutionary thoughts. I turned around.

Max arrived.

15

I was so happy. I almost told Max that the beard suited him. I was ready to hug and kiss him all over. But he wouldn't get it. He didn't know what an unbelievable thought occurred to me, what a realization descended upon me the moment before he showed up.

"What are you so happy about?" Max asked, dusting snow off his hat. "I thought you were tortured. Instead you're having fun? Couldn't wait for me?"

"Max, what are you talking about? What fun?"

"Sanya? Did you get drunk here without me? Shame on you! I'd…"

"Max, stop it," I interrupted. "Eric, excuse me, would you tell him," I pointed my finger at Max, "that I had nothing to drink…"

"Except for cola with lemon and ice," Eric quickly answered. "Are you the gentleman I was giving directions to? Good thing you made it. Your friend nearly fainted. Sitting here all sad. I'm trying to cheer him up a little, telling him stories. And he wouldn't drink," Eric winked at Max and smiled.

"We're about to correct that last part," Max shot back at once and elbowed me. "What are you having?"

Before getting a drink, I glanced at the watch. It was ten to ten. I'm finally drinking with Max. I've been thinking about this for several hours, and now… we're drinking!

A gulp of cognac! A shot each!

Cognac poured inside of me, slipped over the tongue and throat… Oh, how I've wanted this! I've been waiting for the relief. I tossed back the cognac and drank it with such pleasure that somewhere far, far away the flagship of the British Royal Navy saluted as it led a squadron back into the port, exhausted after a long time at sea.

I felt like my body was also happy. Cognac, of course, isn't exactly healthy sleep or regular meals or fresh air. But… it's an option.

16

We each drank a shot of cognac and got ready to leave. I didn't want to stay there another minute. Max agreed. He grumbled, unhappy that I made him come all this way, wasting the precious time of Moscow nightlife just to drink cheap cognac in a ridiculous café. Max and I were arguing when a man who sat at the table by the door approached the bar.

"Here you go, Eric, there is enough there. Thank you!" He said and put the cash on the counter.

"My pleasure! Have a good one!" The bartender smiled.

The man nodded, turned around and met my gaze. Clearly, he recognized me as well and greeted me with a confused nod. I nodded back. He walked off hurriedly.

The interaction wasn't lost on Max, who instantly pressed up against me, looking sideways at the gray-haired man, and asked:

"Is that some famous actor or something?" He whispered.

I wanted to turn around, to look at the man one more time, but Max was already eyeing him. It felt awkward.

"Sanya, introduce me to some famous actors! You promised. Like, who is that guy?" Just then, I heard the door shut behind me. "An actor?"

"I don't know. I can't remember where we met. Maybe he is an actor. God..." I almost raised my voice. "Eric, it looked like you knew that man, the one who just left."

"That one?" Eric poked his finger at that money the man left on the bar before leaving. I nodded. "No, I don't know him. He comes in a lot, maybe works nearby. They all know me around here," he pointed at the tag reading "Eric" on his chest.

"Got it..." I said.

We settled our bill. This time Max let me pay. He wanted to go to some crowded place. He wanted, as he put it, "movement". I kept naming different places and he kept asking: "Sanya, is it a trendy place?" or "Sanya, does it smell of vice?" Having made no decision, we walked outside. The snow fell in large flakes. Fluffy and thick. We came outside, and the first warm wave washed over me. Cognac! It kicked in. The empty stomach and exhaustion accelerated and strengthened this wave. Snow! Freshness and purity...

Moscow instantly became brighter. Windows, streetlights, the lights of billboards and ads were reflected in the low sky and in each of the snowflakes – both soaring and already fallen. "She loves me," I guessed. "I am a good man. It's alright to love me. God... I am good."

I am good... I can do it... I should take a trip home, to my parents... To see them not as a guest from Moscow, for a couple of hours one evening, but stay the entire August, to live with them at the dacha. To sit with my father in the banya, to talk and talk... To take my son to the river... To visit grandma and try not to irritate her, to drink tea with her, hear her out about everything, look at the photos... I should visit my grandpa's grave at the cemetery... Not even to stand at the gravestone, but to try to really think about him. I didn't like it when he used to catch and squeeze me when I was little... I should get together with all my friends, to tell them that I despair without them.

Thinking all this, I took out the phone and dialed a number...

"Hello, Pascal? Hi, it's Sasha," I said into the mouthpiece.

"Sasha. It's so good that you called. I am really not in love with how we departed. I don't speak Russian correctly, you know, I didn't get a chance to explain anything to you. But I understand that you could have taken the wrong way..."

"Pascal! Everything is fine. I am not upset. Forget it! I wanted to thank you myself. You've really helped me. I'm totally unable to keep up with things lately, but didn't have it in me to refuse Alyosha's offer. So everything worked out very well! Forget it!"

"Sasha, is that true? But I think you are mad at me, and you are right..."

"Pascal! I am sorry, let's meet tomorrow and talk about it if you like. But I think there nothing else to talk about. Everything is fine! So I'd rather we talk about something else."

"Wonderful! Tomorrow, of course..."

"Great! I am sort of in a rush, goodbye, take care!"

"Goodbye!" Pascal said hesitantly.

Max was hailing a car. A taxi stopped.

"Sanya, where are we going? The driver is asking, where to?" He shouted.

"Max, wait, I'll be right there, don't let him go." I shouted back. I stood still, holding the phone in my hand and dialing Her number. She answered...

"I am sorry, I know I wasn't supposed to call you," I said in a surprisingly calm voice. "But I couldn't not call. It felt to me like I had to call right now, immediately..." she stayed silent. "I love you so much!!! I can't be without you! There..."

"I know," she said.

She said that... and then there was silence. Several avalanches descended somewhere in the Alps.

"I don't know what else to say," I said steadily, almost in a word.

She also said that she didn't know what else to say. She said that she was waiting... And She also said that it would be easier now to wait until tomorrow, and asked me to call her in the morning.

"Absolutely! Can't wait!" I said.

She said she also... couldn't wait. And then I heard short tones. Completely deaf and shell-shocked, walked over to the taxi, to Max. The snow kept falling, still sheer.

17

When I came up to the taxi, I noticed a car, parked some distance to the left of us. That is, to the left of Max, myself and the taxi. It was a large car, all covered in snow. Suddenly, the window wipers performed their usual semicircle-and-back. It looked like the car opened its eyes. It was the same Mercedes. It's strange, but these Mercedes muzzles never appeared menacing to me. Self-important, pompous, smug, well-fed, boring and sleepy, yes – but never menacing. Because of the amount of snow on top of it, the car has obviously been there for some time.

So what? I decided, I don't care, I have nothing to be afraid of. I got into the taxi with confidence. Let him sit there in his Mercedes like a fool while we get drunk.

"To Miasnitskaya," I told the driver.

Max sat in the front, I in the back. I felt well and relaxed. I knew in advance that the calm wouldn't last long and would abruptly turn to desperation and longing. But not now! Not right now! She said She knew that I loved Her! Said that she waited for me to say it, asked me to call tomorrow! Maybe She couldn't talk right now. But then neither could I. Everything was fine! Everything is fine… We drove slowly. Max was discussing the Moscow weather with the driver and telling him what the winter and frosts were like back in our hometown… "Over there, winter – that's real winter!" He kept saying…

I was awakened by the watchman. He shook me by shoulder and I woke up. I was sleeping at the bottom of a shallow trench. Sand blew in and collected in all the creases of my clothes… It was on my lips too. The young soldier was saying something, but I couldn't tell right away where I was or what was happening. Then I propped myself up against the machine gun, got up, dusted the sand off myself and listened to the watchman.

He said that the scouts returned. Only three of them… My whole body strained and I felt like could crush my own teeth, that's how hard I pressed them together. Not Max!

Seven men had left. Max led them. Four scouts and three diversionists. Three returned… Then, the soldier said that one sergeant was wounded, that a lieutenant and the surviving private carried him on their backs. Also, they brought some important documents…

"The lieutenant returned?" I asked.

The lieutenant returned unharmed. Max returned! I rushed to the tent. There, on the tarpaulin spread right over the sand, lay the wounded man. He was being bandaged with fresh bandages. Sitting at the table were Max and another scout. They were surrounded by about ten men from my platoon. A gas lamp burned bright on the table, folders, notebooks and an open binder with a map were scattered nearby.

"Hey, stranger! You knew I wouldn't come back without treats," Max said to me. "Look what else was in the box with this crap."

By crap he meant folders and documents, which he struggled to bring back with immense difficulty and at the cost of four men's lives… Max pulled a pack of cigars out of the bag. It was white, with yellow corners and edges… It was more appetizing than a box of chocolates. Cigars!

"Max, we've got to talk, let's step aside."

We stepped aside and, as briefly as possible, I explained the situation. Max was very tired and drained from the two days that he'd been gone. I was happy. First of all, Max was back. Secondly, turned out I was right to insist that somebody stay back. And thirdly, Max had obtained some important intelligence, which meant that my platoon would not die in vain come morning. Now we had to decide how to deliver the documents, maps and the wounded soldier… meaning, how to catch up with the retreating battalion.

"No, mate, I can't think about that right now. I have to eat something and get some sleep, at least an hour," said Max.

"Negative. You have to leave immediately, there isn't more than an hour and a half left to sunrise. You must make it to…"

"Who told you I was going anywhere? I brought back what I found, what you do with it is up to you guys. I am tired. I need some sleep."

"Max, you must…"

"You're in command of the rifle platoon, so go and command!" He cut me off. "Me, I am intelligence. I am going to sleep. I've tired myself out like a dog while you were cooling off here. I'll sleep, meanwhile you ship the papers and the wounded... Then wake me up, we'll smoke the cigars. And if you haven't finished your prized whiskey, we'll drink it – then back to war. But for now, sleep. Sleep!"

He went back to the tent, leaving me behind. I stood watching him go and smiled.

There were still many cars out on the road. Friday evening, Moscow... Everyone is searching, searching for something!

The car windows were fogged up, windshield wipers working at maximum speed. I kept turning around trying to spot those familiar headlights. No. Nothing definitive, yet for some reason I was absolutely certain that my pursuer was following us.

"Yeah. Minus forty-five is better than the slush you've got here," Max was telling the driver. "Dry cold. All the germs and viruses freeze. No flu. Beautiful...!"

"Max, stop piling on, will you?" I inserted. "How many times did it drop down to minus forty-five last winter? A polar bear over here! Don't listen to him. Here, pull over right here, please..."

I paid for the ride, but Max shoved some cash into the driver's hand as well. We stepped out of the taxi. The front of the establishment was jammed with expensive cars. People powdered with snow stood by the door. It meant there was no room inside. I looked around – a long queue of cars slowly crawled up the snowed in street. I didn't see the Mercedes.

"Is this a trendy place?" Asked Max.

"Quite trendy, can't you tell? People are lining up to get in."

"Do famous actors come here?"

"Sometimes."

"Introduce me?"

"Max!"

"How are we going to get in?"

"I've got some pull," I said and started looking for the club's business card in my wallet.

"Is there vice in there?" Max continued.

"There will be, as soon as we get it," I answered.

Still, I knew that Max wouldn't like it too much. Which is not to suggest that Max is into gypsy debauchery or Russian chanson. It's just that we were going into a trendy and therefore somewhat boring establishment. But I really needed a drink and soon! Didn't matter where. And Max wanted "trendy". No problem!

We squeezed between those awaiting their chance to get in. I showed a business card to a large bouncer. He carefully looked at me, at Max and... let us in. His face didn't change, he simply stopped looking at us. Inside, we were met by a similar-looking fellow... "I wonder, where do they make such bad suits for these guys?" I thought.

There weren't as many people inside as it seemed from the outside. Indian music was playing, all waiters dressed in Indian-style outfits. Three very attractive women were waiting for their tokens by the coat check. Max stared at them.

"Terrific!" Said Max. "So are we a couple of Ernest's tonight or did we come in to take a piss?"

"I don't know, we'll see. Though I'm afraid there isn't enough of me left to play Ernest tonight. It's Friday, Max. People went out full of hope, determined to stay up till morning. I don't think I can go on Hemingwaying that long."

"But can we find vice here?"

"You look for it, Max! You know that smell better than I do."

We checked our coats, got our tokens. I ended up with number 27. I liked it. It pleased me. A good number. Max got a number 46 – nonsense.

We were seated quickly. It wasn't the best table, but it allowed for a good view.

"Look, Sanya! Check it out!" Max bulged his eyes and pointed somewhere behind me. I turned around and saw a bunch of polished-looking men and a pair of women.

"Who?" I asked.

"That one, in a tan suit. It's that famous... what's his face... Economist, I think... Yes! Economist or political pundit."

"Max, the hell with him! They're all over the place."

"No, it's great! Just that it's nice to know that we're in a place that famous people come to. So what are we drinking? You order this time."

"You got it, Max. I know just what to order."

"Sanya, ask them or for something trendy."

"First strong, then trendy, alright?"

EVGENY GRISHKOVETS

"Excellent!" Max kept brushing his knees with his hands and looking around with a glistening gaze.

We instantly had a shot of tequila each and ordered a couple of large mojitos.

"What's a mojito?" Max inquired. "Is it trendy?"

"Trendy. And has been for a long time. You'll like it," I assured him.

After a while, Max spotted a couple of famous businessmen at the next table, some athlete and an actress from television. I exchanged greetings with a couple of acquaintances. Max was pleased. The music played loudly, but not too loudly... I wasn't as much relaxed as I was in the middle of everything. That is, slightly apart from it. I tried to force myself not to think, not to analyze Her last words.

Max languidly leafed through the menu. Indian dishes and their names amused him. He read them out loud – dishes whose strange names told him nothing about their ingredients – and laughed. "Like an old man," I thought.

"Let's smoke some cigars," Max suddenly offered.

I was surprised. I remembered my last vision; they no longer baffled me... "Isn't that something?" I thought.

"Max, have you looked at the prices? The night is young."

"Sanya, again with the money? It's my treat! When you come back to visit, you'll treat everyone, but tonight I am the big daddy. Let's get some cigars!"

I love to smoke cigars. Just smoking, as in regular cigarettes, that I have managed to quit recently. I used to smoke in the army, then quit. Off a bet. I took bets seriously back in those days. At twenty-five, sure! But I only started smoking cigars recently, once already in Moscow. Not often. I didn't turn into a cigar connoisseur, but I'd have one sometimes... for pleasure...

"Let's smoke. Why not?"

So I asked for the cigars.

They brought us the humidor (a box for keeping cigars).

Here is the conversation Max and I had about cigars.

Max: Sanya, which one should pick? I don't know a damn thing about them.

Me: Pick the one you like.

Max: I don't like any of them, that's what I'm saying, I don't know anything about them.

Me: No? Buy one you like, I mean one that looks best to you… you know, by appearance. The one that smiles at you, that's the one to grab.

Max: Are they Cubans, not Cubans – isn't that important or what?

Me: Sure, it's important. Everything is important! But it's such a wilderness, this cigar business. It's better not delve too deeply into it. Books written about cigars alone, there are so many…! So just take one that looks best to you on the outside, and you won't go wrong.

Max: This one. *(Max pointed at the thickest and longest cigar.)* A good one, I think! *(The young woman holding the cigars smiled.)*

Me *(almost smirked)*: A good one. But you'll croak from it. You won't finish it in an hour.

Max: Even better. What's the rush?

Me: It's the strongest cigar. Take that one instead.

Max: See? First you tell me to pick one myself and then, as always, slip me something else. No, I'm taking the one I like.

Me: Max, don't be stubborn.

Max: Enough. I'm taking the one I like. Let me suffer.

Me: Everyone is going to suffer from that smoke… But you know what? *(I waved him off.)* It's pointless arguing with you…

Max: Exactly! Pointless. Let me relax, please. Sanya… which one did you pick?

Me *(I selected a cigar of average size and strength.)*: This one.

Max: And why?

Me: Just because… I like it. *(I let the young woman with the cigars go.)*

Max: By the look of it?

Me: Well… I like this one specifically. I've smoked it before… And I like it.

Max: But what's the difference?

Me: There's a big difference. That's what I'm telling you, it's all complicated. If take this subject seriously… basically, it's just this whole big to-do.

Max: No, just explain to me why you like it. Tastes good, or what?

Me: Well… yeah, actually. I'd say yes, it does taste good.

Max: And what, mine doesn't?

Me: Max, they all taste good. But differently… That's obvious. They're all made with different tobacco, rolled differently, come from different places, in different shapes. I'm not an expert either. If you seriously get into this... like I said – it's this whole big subject!

Max: And how... how do I do this? *(Max was trying to cut off the cigar.)*

Me: Let me do that myself. *(I took the guillotine for cutting cigars away from Max.)* You see, these cigars are generally fun and expensive toys. And everything that has to do with them – basically the same thing, fun and expensive toys for men. Here! *(I showed Max the guillotine.)* There's a shitload of different ones. This kind and that, some made of gold... By the way, this a box for cigars...

Max: It has a funny name, doesn't it?

Me: A humidor.

Max: A what?

Me: A humidor. Not to be confused with pompadour. They too can get really expensive! They're supposed to preserve a certain level of humidity, they even install a special device for this... Keeping different cigars in the same box is not recommended... and so on. And it's all expensive...

Max: Damn it! *(Max started coughing.)*

Me: Don't inhale it.

Max: Yeah, I know! Just doesn't work. I automatically inhale like *(coughing)*. Mother of...!

Me: I told you.

Max: Sanya, this paper here *(Max pointed at the decorative paper ring encircling the cigar.)* Am I supposed to remove it?

Me: That I'm not sure about exactly. Sometimes I take it off, sometimes I don't. Do as you like.

Max: As I like? *(Max carefully removed the little paper ring from the cigar and put it on his finger, then stretched out his hand and admired how it fit.)*

Me: *(after small pause)* Cigars – they are definitely delicious!

Max: I don't get it. I think it's all pure show off. But sure, it looks impressive. *(He expelled a whole cloud of smoke from his mouth.)*

Me: No, you're wrong. A good cigar, right atmosphere... delicious! The effect is... like from good cognac or whiskey... Sure, it's not exactly the same, but just as palpable.

Max: Then what's the difference? Drink cognac and that's it... works faster and better.

Me: Hang on, Max. If that's the case... then why drink cognac? You can just drink vodka – same forty percent by volume. Everything else is just showing off.

Max: Of course it's showing off! Except it's a kind of nice, pricey showing off. It's all showing off, Sanya. But I like it. I'll have to figure out this cigar business.

Me: Oh, come on! What do you need to figure out cigars for? It's not like you'll be smoking them all the time. There is really no difference between us... We're both caricatures with these cigars... caricatures of ourselves. No matter how many books you read about these cigars, no matter how much you learn about them... Just look at yourself with a cigar! Your beard, a cigar... This is how they portray evil Americans in those Indian movies.

Max: Yeah? I don't care! I would buy a hat to go with it too...

Me: Why not a sombrero? Bolder still, more uncompromising...

Max: Idiot. Hats actually look good on me...

Me: They look good on everyone. I'd wear one myself. Not to be provocative or strange, but just because... you know? It's just that nowadays almost nobody wears them... which is why it would seem... not immodest, but... something more than just wearing a hat. More than just because! And I just want to wear a hat and not think that I'm wearing one.

Max: Things are pretty twisted up in your head, aren't they? My goodness! What's up with you? *(Max shook his head.)* So are you saying that everybody wears neckerchiefs?

Me: The neckerchief – that was a gift. And there are reasons why I have it around my neck, since...

Max: A gift? In that case, give me a hat as a gift. I'll wear it tell and everybody that it was a gift from you. That way, all that ridicule is on somebody else, not me. By the way *(Max narrowed his eyes)*, how's my flashlight? Did she like it?

Me: No, Max... I mean, I didn't give it to her yet. Here, you can have it back. *(I put the flashlight on the table.)*

Max: Give me a break. It felt good to buy it. And that's enough for me. *(Max grew noticeably sadder or, to be more precise, stopped being happy.)*

And that was the chat Max and I had about cigars.

"So you called me over there," Max motioned his hand indeterminately, implying the small café on the Avenue of Peace, "because she never showed up?"

"Yes, Max. Exactly."

He nodded several times. That's when they brought the mojitos. Max was clearly impressed by what they placed on the table in front of him. He stuck a straw in his mouth and took a few sips.

"Tasty," he said. "No really, this is seriously tasty. I like it," he took a silent pause. "So I guess you're really in love? Lucky you. What do you think, those over there, think we can play with them? Let's Hemingway a bit."

Max pointed at the three beauties that we saw by the coat check. Now all three were sitting at their table, discussing something cheerfully.

"Tell me, Sanya, why is it that all women, whenever they go out somewhere at night, they always act like this?" He pointed a finger at them. "It's not like they put on fancy clothes, fuss in front of the mirror for each other, right? They came here to meet somebody… right or wrong? So why the hell do they always sit there acting like they don't need anybody and that they're having such fun? Why, Sanya?"

"It's a rhetorical question, Max. We won't be playing Ernest's with those ladies. Nothing will come of it."

"Why's that? I have a beard, a cigar. Sanya, if you don't want to, I'll try on my own."

"Don't even try. It will make for very unpleasant memories. These girls wait and wait, but not for you. They know how we got here, they scanned for how you're dressed, how you carry yourself, how you hold that cigar, what table we were seated at… Your only chance to chat with them is if they don't meet anyone else by two in the morning. After two – go ahead and try."

"You're wrong, Sanya. These aren't working girls. Why do you…"

"Who said they were working girls? Of course not! Max, things aren't that primitive, but not terribly complicated either. These girls… basically, they're status girls… And you just don't have the right status."

"Nonsense! I am a fun, good-natured and kind man. That's already enough to…"

"And they, Max, are boring, cheerless and unkind. So spending time, energy and money on them is a waste. That's right, money too! They won't appreciate it. They're used to it. They make me sick…"

My phone rang. I jolted and spilled some of the cocktail on my chest. But I didn't curse, I feverishly searched for the phone inside the pocket of my jacket… It was Pascal.

"Sasha-a-á! I am calling you because I love you!" I could hear that Pascal was calling from some loud place. He was shouting into the receiver and was genuinely drunk. "Come to us, please!"

"Pascal! How did you get drunk so fast, it's only…"

"Sashá! I can't hear," he kept shouting.

"Just a minute," I shouted back. "Sorry, Max, I'll be right back." I said to Max.

I got up from the table and walked off to the door, where the music was quieter and I didn't disturb anybody.

"Sashá! Come soon if you want to see me, and if you want me to still recognize you, come! It is fun here!"

"Pascal, you didn't waste time getting wasted! Good man!"

"Yes! I am good man! Sashá, I love you! I am such a scum, and you are my friend! Here we talk only about you!"

"My boy, if you are there with Katya, be careful. Watch yourself… Try not to be alone with her without witnesses."

"I understand, I am trying… Therefore, I drink! Come soon!"

"No, Pascal! Let's reconnect tomorrow. Go have fun without me."

"Alright! I understand! No one needs an old drunk French person. Bye!"

"Be careful there! Bye!"

I stood by the window. The snow was falling not so heavily now, big flakes becoming lighter. Each one flew separately. On the other side of the window, the wind swirled oddly and the snow flew upwards. I watched it for a minute. Then just glanced toward the street. The familiar Mercedes was parked on the other side. Its hazards flashed and smoke was coming out of the tailpipe, and the interior was dark. Whoever was inside was warming up. "I should discuss this with Max, his brain is better wired than mine when it comes to such things," I decided and went back to the table.

Max wasn't there. I checked around and spotted him at the corner table. He was kissing the hand of a skinny woman with a very expressive face and a long, powerful neck. She was chortling and saying something to Max. Her companion, a bald man in a fitted white sweater, was laughing heartily. Max bowed at everyone, said something else, backed away, waved playfully and returned to the table, beaming.

"There!" He said and put a piece of paper ripped out of a notebook on the table. "If you're not going to introduce me to famous people, I'll introduce myself."

"What is that?" I asked, pointing at the paper.

"An autograph! I told her I was her fan. I asked her to give me some other personal item too. And she did!" He displayed a cheap plastic lighter.

I picked up the paper and read: "Gosha! All the best to you! To you and your friends!" An indistinct signature followed.

"Gosha? Who is that? Would that be you, Gosha?" I inquired.

"No! Gosha is you!" Max spoke in a loud conspiratorial whisper. "You and I, we came here from far away, where we have her fan club in our city. And you love her work so much that you were too shy to approach her and even left out of nervousness. So take the paper. It's for you."

"Fool," I said calmly, took the paper, faced the table where the actress sat, found her gaze, kissed the scrap ceremoniously and put it in the inside pocket of my jacket. She laughed.

"Good man," Max commended me, took the straw out of his glass, silently ordered me to do the same, clanged glasses with me and drank the remains of his cocktail, sipping the liquid through ice, much of it still deposited at the bottom of the glass. I repeated every detail after him.

"Sanya, you better button up your jacket. You look like a drunken aristocrat." Max whispered.

I glanced at my shirt. A mojito stain was just starting to dry on my chest. The cocktail is obviously colorless… still, it was awkward. A dark brown stain could be seen on my chest. Not large, but noticeable. I must have put it there when I sat pressing against the bar… back there… at the café. I buttoned the jacket. Hid the brown stain.

"Soiled, aren't we, your excellency?" I told myself.

18

I told Max about the Mercedes. He instantly turned more serious and thoroughly interrogated me about all the details. Then we went up to the window to have a look. The Mercedes was still there. Max took a couple of minutes to think. We returned to the table and he order anther couple of mojitos.

"Sanya, this is great! A fucking adventure! Great!" Max was genuinely happy. "Oh, if only we were back home, I'd call the guys, they'd run his license plates... We'd know whose car this is in ten minutes. But in Moscow, who do you call?"

"Here is what I don't get, Max. How could they find me on Vernadsky Avenue? I took the metro there. Do I have a hundred people tailing me, or what? Think about it, who am I to...?"

"It's simple! Find out where your sites are and how many you have – simple as that. Go to first, second, third..."

"I have two of them."

"Even better! And what does that mean: 'Who am I?' Sure, you're not an enemy of the state or stealing money from the mafia. If you were, they'd be looking for you differently. You wouldn't know about it. But in this case, you've got somebody driving the same car and not hiding much. Doesn't look like someone's trying to scare you either. Most likely, a jealous husband."

"She is not married..."

"Then a guy... Some boyfriend. It's simple! But whose boyfriend, that I wouldn't know."

What Max was saying was logical, but strange. We'd met only four times. Always at some daytime hour... In other words, not late and not for too long. Maybe She told someone about me... but not likely. She wouldn't give out my name, address and place of work. If She did something like that, she'd certainly warn me about it. I shared my doubts with Max, but admitted that his hypothesis was the most productive. No wonder, as soon as I saw the Mercedes, I started to worry about Her.

"We'll figure it out, Sanya. Everything is fine! Here we are, in a trendy place, amid famous actresses, drinking! And he is sitting there smoking in his car. Serves him right. He is worse off than we are. Don't fret, we'll take care of it tonight and have some fun too. I've got to tell you, Sanya, you're the man! You really are! Stylish, successful man, head over heels in love, and somebody is following you! This is super!"

"Max, does this put Her in any danger?"

Max twisted his lips, squinted and took fifteen seconds or so to think.

"I doubt it," he said finally. "If she knew or sensed something like that, she'd warn you, like you said. And you would have probably picked up on it too if something were off," Max narrowed his eyes and smiled. "You fell in love for real, Sanya! Tell me about her. I'm so curious!"

"Max, I'll have another drink and then tell you, but now…"

"Oh, come on! She isn't all that interesting to me per se. In fact, I don't even want to meet her in person. It's not like I'll be able to see her with your eyes. So I'll see a woman who's got my friend all shaking, tormented. And what? What do I need to see her for? It's better that you tell me about her. That's more interesting. You are more interesting to me. And the woman tormenting you, absolutely…"

"Tormenting? What're you talking about?" I couldn't stand it. "No one has ever treated me with more care. She is real! She is so real…"

"Sanya, you misunderstood me. Real, real! There you go, harping on the same thing. I don't need real." Max was being more than serious. "I know what 'real' means. And I don't want to hear about that. I mean, look… three days ago, I'm sitting in my kitchen. At night. We had some drinks at dinner. With the guys. Not much. I get home, sit in the kitchen alone, drinking tea, sobering up. And suddenly I get this powerful feeling that life is real, you know! Life – it's a real thing!" I've rarely seen Max so serious. "I mean, I'm sitting in the kitchen, drinking tea. There is kitchen furniture, tile, refrigerator, window, it's dark out there, night. I am already over thirty. I am real! In the morning, at ten, I have to go to a meeting to negotiate prices for cinder blocks. I need lots of them, so I'll be asking to let them go for less. Fucking cinder blocks! Understand? They're real. Neither bad nor good, but real. And I'm sitting in the kitchen, drinking tea. Drinking boiled water with dried leaves… Sanya, life is real! I understood this and… and it bummed me out! Because… is it all for THIS? Just don't oversimplify what I've just told you. I told myself that life was real. It doesn't mean that life is pointless, that it's all nonsense and we're just bullshiting around. No, Sanya! That would be too simple! But that life is real… REAL! Which is more frightening… So I came here. And here you've got intrigue, love, Moscow! Sanya, you don't even realize how lucky you are."

"Me, lucky? And life is real?" I said in a sufficiently steady voice. "How come what you're saying to me sounds like some sort of reproach?"

At first, I even wanted to object, to say that I wasn't lucky. Why is it that any time somebody tells you that you're lucky, you always have to justify yourself. To say, no, I'm not lucky – or yes, I am lucky, but I've got this and that, or some ache or something. And then they respond that they too have aches, and you say that yours are still worse…

Just then we got our mojitos. We clinked glasses, nodded to each and took a few sips.

"So, go on…" Max encouraged me.

"So anyway! I don't know if I'm lucky or not. Even when things are great, I don't know if that's luck or happiness or not. Maybe that's exactly what it is. But I don't know it. I imagine that, maybe, it could be much better. Otherwise, I am happy, sure, but always in some specific way. Is that really happiness? I actually don't remember ever being happy. There have been times when I felt great, really great, in fact. But happy…? I remember applying to the university. I was taking enrollment exams, I was nervous, and before that I would visit the university, look around, then I'd submitted my documents and thought: 'Is it possible that I'm going to be a student, just like these wonderful people sitting in auditoriums and smoking in hallways?' I couldn't believe it. And then I read my last name on the list of those accepted. It was such a relief! I called my parents with the good news, came outside and took a walk. It was summertime, I bought ice-cream. I was walking, a big phase of my life had come to end. And now, full speed ahead…! Freedom, interesting work and people, a wonderful life! I was walking and felt really, really good. But had I known then that my life would never feel better, then maybe, at that moment, I could have felt happiness. And today I can say that I know what is and what it feels like to be happy."

EVGENY GRISHKOVETS

Max was listening very seriously and carefully. If not for his stupid beard, one could even say that he was amazed – such a thoughtful and intense face he had in that moment. Our cigars went out and, without conspiring to do so, we each lit them up again.

"Max, you tell me life is real? Of course! Life is hyperreal! I mean, I fell in love, right? But when I look at Her, I do see Her for real! More real than anybody else. She is very beautiful! So beautiful that I don't even know what I want. I love Her so much that I am incapable of wanting. But last time, when I was coming to meet her, I thought: 'If only I could hold Her hand and talk to Her – that's all! I don't need anything else. I don't want anything else. Because what could be greater than sitting next to Her and holding Her hand?' And so we meet, sit across from each other. Between my eyes and Hers, there are maybe fifty-sixty centimeters at most. Her hands are on the table... so are mine. And suddenly, She touches my hand, and I put mine on Hers... And we sat like that! But as soon as that happened, the moment my hand lay over Hers... at that precise moment, THAT was no longer enough. Instantly! You see, not a second of happiness! And it only became harder and more painful..."

"Sanya, that's because you fell in love! For real... And me, I don't fall in love, Sanya. At all!"

I'd known Max for more than ten years. We met when I already finished university while he was on his third year. He wasn't at the same university. He was studying with my then future and now ex-wife. They were studying economics. By then, like me, he'd already served in the army. We became instant friends, our friendship an intense one. Max would constantly fall in love and, as a result, perform all kinds of extraordinary things, always with a certain flare.

Suddenly, the club manager approached us and pointed out a man standing by the entrance. He was dressed in a colorful sweater and jeans tucked into short winter boots.

"Gentlemen," the manager said. "That man over there," he pointed at the man in the sweater, "has something for you. He would like to return something to you. Unfortunately, because of the way he is dressed, we asked him to wait by the..."

"Whoa!" Max exclaimed abruptly. "No way!"

Max rushed to this man, ran up to him, cheerfully shook his hand and led him out of my field of vision. He returned a minute later, carrying his new briefcase.

"Sanya! That was the taxi guy who drove us here. Imagine, I tossed the briefcase in the back seat and left it there. You're obviously of no use, would probably leave your head somewhere the state you're in now, out of your mind… But he spotted it and, see? Came back. Wouldn't take the money. I barely convinced him. See what kind of people come along sometimes? What a guy! A native Muscovite, and still…"

19

Amazing! How could it be? Max got his briefcase back. But I never got my gloves back. What sort of a man was that? A nice and very pleasant taxi driver, he saw where I came out. Clearly, I was headed to a restaurant. He could've dropped off the gloves. But no! And Max gets his briefcase? What's going on?

We finished our mojitos and I flatly refused to drink more. I just didn't want to... I wasn't thirsty. Besides, I realized why it wasn't hitting me. It was time to move up to stronger drinks, only I didn't want to stay there. There was no point. What for? They were about to turn up the volume. The place was filling up. The hardcore nighttime people were about to arrive, but what would be the point in watching them? The people who come out to raid Moscow at night were full of purpose. Sure, purposes can vary, but a person driven by a purpose is a bad companion for two guys over thirty out for a night with no specific purpose. They just want to tire themselves enough to fall fast asleep and sleep without dreaming.

"Come on, this won't work," Max said and leaned back in his chair. "I can't party by myself. Sanya, I've been dying to come see you in Moscow, thought we'd let ourselves go here..." Max clutched his fists and shook them, "I could've philosophized back home. There is so much possibility here, and you're sitting here all sour."

"Just don't tell me I've become spoiled, alright?"

"Of course you're spoiled! Just imagine how many people would be happy just to get in here... to sit in this classy place, among famous people. But for you all it is now is, you know, nothing special. So yes, you're spoiled."

About fifteen years ago, I took a summer vacation in Sochi. I was just starting to earn money and decided to spend the summer by the sea, invited my ex-wife to come with my son. The vacation turned out to be pretty tense, but we – meaning my former wife and I – kept up the appearance of an ideal relationship in front of our son. Those who observed us would've concluded that we were a wonderful, inseparable couple. We, for our part, were proud of our tolerance and grace. On the outside, everything was quite touching, yet there was not a single night, like in those American movies, when, after a breakup, a man and a woman reunite by some seashore and spend a long day... They have casual lunch together and toss crumpled paper napkins or salad greens at each other playfully, then go into the water and frolic in the waves, and after that, ride carousels or shoot air guns for stuffed toys, music is playing amid the evening lights and the joy of a little seaside town, and later at dusk they open a bottle of champagne in their hotel room, where he asks in a whisper, holding her by the shoulders: "Do you think we should try one more time... a fresh start?" And after that... you know!

Max visited me in Sochi. Said nothing and surprised me...

Late at night we heard a terrible noise and thunderous scuffling in the hotel hallway. I was nodding off in front of the TV, my son was asleep, my ex-wife next to him reading. And suddenly, someone screamed bloody murder. I ran out of the room and saw it: Max trying to push through the security guards – and he did... Apparently, he'd already encountered resistance downstairs, but he was able to break through and lured the guards behind him. He had a cone on his head, a blue one, with sparkling stars. In one hand, he held a bottle of champagne, in the other a bunch of balloons. They kept popping and their tatters dangled on the threads. Max was totally red, drunk and quite determined. There were two drunk girls with him. They were giggling and wearing costumes. One was dressed up as Little Red Riding Hood. Upon seeing me, Max rejoiced, but I betrayed him. I renounced him and even scolded him. To this day, I cannot forgive myself for that. Even though one might understand where I was coming from. I'd spent a whole two weeks displaying magnanimity... at the start of August... in Sochi! And then this comet of freedom and abandon comes flying in...

"So, where should we go? Why keep sitting here like this?" Asked Max. "Sanya, don't get so sour. I got up today around four in the morning, Moscow time. If our party keeps going like this, I'm going to fall asleep. If we're not going to play Hemingway tonight, then at least let me find love. Don't get in the way. Seeing as you are now in a frenzy, I can't hang my hopes on you. Or let's drink already. Just drink! We've got to decide what to do. I'd love to eat something, but not here."

He had barely smoked a third of his cigar. We asked for the check and another round of tequilas. We drank it, Max paid, then carefully wrapped the remains of his cigar in a napkin and handed it to me.

"Take it, Sanya, put in the pocket of your jacket."

"I won't be finishing your cigar."

"I'm not offering. It's my cigar! I'll be smoking till morning. Put it in your pocket, or I'll end up squishing it. You're the neat one."

"I will not. My whole jacket will stink of tobacco."

"What I am supposed to do, keep holding it in my hand or what?"

"Max, what about the briefcase?"

Max slapped himself on the forehead, took the briefcase, put the cigar inside and got up to go.

"Hold on," I stopped him, "sit down. Let's decide where to go. Instead of running back and forth in the cold, let's map out a plan first."

"Let's do it." Max sat back down.

"What, 'let's do it'? Decide what you want."

"Sanya, this won't work either," Max said seriously. "If you don't feel like doing anything at all, let's be on our merry way and go to sleep. Otherwise, you'll be escorting me with your sour muzzle like some dog walker. What do I need that kind of fun for?"

"You're right, Max. Sorry… Alright… I'm just thinking of the best place to go. I wouldn't mind drinking some more, either. But not too much! I have to be in excellent shape in the morning. She and I agreed we'd talk on the phone tomorrow."

My heart leapt up and froze from joy for a few moments. I remembered our telephone conversation. She asked me to call her! She knows that I love her! My heart returned to its place and I and was able to speak again.

"Right now is the time when everything is about to begin. We could make it to some club for a concert, we could go to one where there is dancing… but it's loud there, and I don't want to lose my voice shouting over the music. We could go to a casino. Could play pool, bowling…"

"Sanya, every backward village is full of this stuff nowadays. Casino, pool, bowling. Big deal! Bowling! People do it thinking it's an actual sport and that's actually healthy. They smoke and drink there, thinking to themselves: 'We play sports and take care of ourselves.' Everybody's face is so serious in bowling… You've got a bowling player, ass and belly the size of bowling balls, standing there holding a ball, a cigarette in his teeth, squinting, assuming his pose, as if concentrating…"

"You don't like bowling? Forget it. Let's go to banya."

"Banya? No way, I'll definitely fall asleep there."

"Fine, let's got to a strip club."

"Sanya, a strip club? What do you take me for? I didn't just come back from the sea or get out of prison. Let's go to a concert."

"Let's go, but right now. Up and go."

And that's what we did. It was just after eleven – a typical time for club concerts to begin on Friday nights. But they often start a little later. The crowds linger, wait. Then, the musicians come out…

It's a good thing that Max opted for a concert. I haven't been to a concert in a long time. There was a time when I would go to some a concert at a ckyv every week and be amazed by how much is happening in Moscow.

A concert! That's great! I love concerts…

I love to go to the movies… Love it when the film is about to start, a sequence of loud and well-known music comes on, the main title shows up on the screen – a movie studio emblem, and then silence, a dark screen, letters begin to appear and a voice announces something like: "Paramount Pictures Presents…" Music and colors of that first scene burst into the theater: New York, ablaze in lights, a helicopter is soaring… The thrill of anticipation takes hold of your chest… like back in childhood…

We walked up to the coat check and handed in our tokens. That's when the restaurant manager called us.

"Gentleman! You forgot this…" in his outstretched arm, he held a burgundy leather briefcase.

20

We went outside. We left the establishment and two young girls with a guy were shown to our table. They cheerfully leapt inside from the cold while we took to the street. The Mercedes set off after us.

"He is really not hiding. What a fool! Let's go, Sanya," Max said, looking at the Mercedes.

We walked a bit further and caught a taxi. I decided that it was best to go to 16 Tons, an old club, which has always had concerts each Friday and Saturday and where one didn't have to worry about running into something too adolescent. Meaning some teenage music.

Once again, we were driving through Moscow. While we sat in that warm place for a little over an hour, the cold had gotten slightly worse, the snow descended languidly and fancily – languidly and not too densely. Snowplows have already crawled out to the city... But the city wasn't ready to sleep. Moscow sparkled with all of its lights and stirred with thousands of cars moving through it. There were some three weeks left until the New Year, but signs of anticipation of that night could be seen everywhere. In fact, winter itself was only just beginning, the snow would be around for another four months, but Moscow had already grown tired of winter... and maybe that's why everyone was having fun so desperately....

The Mercedes kept following us, but by then I was somehow used to it. Besides, Max was with me and I felt completely safe... I felt relaxed.

Somehow, we made our way to the club. Some Swedish band with an English name was giving a concert. The name told me nothing, but there were many people there, people who knew what they were in for. Moscow! Where you can always find a few hundred fans of anything.

The first floor was mostly occupied by a small number of beer drinkers who sat in front of televisions watching some sport. The rest were pushing their way upstairs. We were still jostling downstairs when we heard that the concert had started. At first, there were loud screams – the musicians must have walked out on stage – then came the sound of music. We rushed.

We didn't feel like squeezing our way to the stage and got stuck in the middle of the ballroom, pressed tightly from all sides. There were two very young guys on the stage. Skinny, with sloping shoulders, stooped, strange… Both were standing in front of control panels with buttons, not looking at the audience, not moving to the beat of the music. It did appear like they were performing some complex and responsible work. The music was very powerful… The first… (I wouldn't call it a song. A composition…? Not really… A piece? What kind of a piece is that? More like a work!) The first work ended and the audience greeted the musicians quite warmly. Max roared in my ear that he'd try to get us drinks and pushed in the direction of the bar.

One of the musicians stepped away from his control panel and picked up a guitar, the other – wearing army fatigue pants, a tank top with a Swedish flag, and a thin, long neck and small closely cropped head – started saying something in English. They audience understood what he was saying. He must have joked twice, and twice they laughed. I thought: "Yeah, I should definitely brush up on my English! One has to be lazy not to know this language."

I studied English in school and at the university, but… not enough. While traveling abroad, I spoke it and could even leaf a newspaper in English. But I didn't understand jokes.

I stood, pressed in tightly by young people. Not that I am old myself, but the people around me were younger… so were the musicians on stage. The closely-cropped one finished speaking and started to play. Very beautiful, powerful, its low sound pressed the audience even tighter. The opening was strikingly impressive. Then came the guitar, piercing right through the most tender part of me… the electric bass followed, succeeded by the percussions… "Fucking Scandinavians!" I thought. I was very impressed. Very powerful…! Then the fellow with the long neck began to sing... He had a pretty feeble, but clean voice… He sang beautifully… Meaning, the way he needed to. The way I needed him to at that moment…

It was almost morning when we found Max's vessel… Once again, the wind was brisk, and we had to work our hardest… This old tub of

EVGENY GRISHKOVETS

Max's was living out its final hours. It tipped hard and was drifting, all beat up by the storm. There was nothing left of the mast, the glass of the wheelhouse was broken, lifeboats apparently torn out and carried away... For three hours, risking terribly and freezing from the wind and splash, we extracted the crew along with the most valuable scientific equipment from the ill-fated vessel. Max was, of course, the last to leave the dying ship. His head was bandaged, icicles dangling from the thick shovel that was his beard, his eyes unbelievably tired.

We rescued everybody. Twelve people: eight sailors, including Max, and four scientists. They were frozen stiff and deadly tired. My crew was busy with everyone but Max. Max, barely standing, remained on the bridge.

We set back on the home-bound course. I contacted land, reported Max's rescue, said the hell with pride and requested help myself. Given the state of our boat, there were plenty of chances not to make it... anywhere. Then Max and I stepped down to my cabin, I took the bottle of brandy from the safe and handed it to Max. He opened it in silence and drank from the bottle. He drank brandy like lukewarm tea, then pulled away from the bottle, wiped his beard with the sleeve of his sweater and passed the bottle back to me...

"Sanya, here," Max roared in my ear and passed me a heavy stubbed glass tumbler.

"What's that?" I asked about the contents of the glass.

"Whiskey!" Max winked and clinked his equally heavy glass with mine.

"Sanya! I'm going downstairs. This music isn't for me. I'll wait for you on the first floor, might try to tangle somebody up."

"Alright! Just don't tangle anybody up for me!" I roared back. By "tangle somebody up" he meant women...

Max nodded back and disappeared while I tuned back into the song, which played and played. The young Swede sang and I thought: "If I could compose songs and music, I would compose this song...! And I would sing it..."

It took some six hours for us to spot the first vessel... A small, but quite new Swedish trawler spotted us first. We radioed the captain. My English was sufficient enough to explain that we were still afloat, that none of those rescued onboard require urgent care, but I did request that they accompany us to the nearest port, just in case. The Swedes eagerly agreed and wished us luck.

I took three good sips of whiskey. Max brilliantly decided on whiskey and brilliantly left. "He is just generally brilliant," I concluded.

I really love music. I always have. Even back in school, roughly in seventh grade, I started to seriously listen to music. I often argued with friends, insisted that the best musicians were, of course, the ones that were my favorite. I would stand up to my parents for my right to listen to my own music... and would hassle them for money... for my own music.

I'd often bring friends to my house, put on some new album of one band or another for them. I'd play my favorite piece and my poor friend would have to sit and listen to guitar solos or rhythmic sketches that I loved. The peach fuzz all over my body would stand up and chills would run up and down my spine from demonstrating my favorite music to somebody else. My senses would intensify from letting somebody else listen to what I really loved. My poor friends... they suffered.

We used what strength we had to reach a small Swedish island. There was only a small fishing village on that island. We were greeted very warmly. We used our own resources to repair my old tub. Those we rescued – the sailors and scientists – were helicoptered by the Swedes onto a large depot ship, which was passing not far from our island.

The island had a single pub where all the local and foreign sailors would gather. Each night, Max and I went there, drank a little vodka with smoked salmon fish soup and potatoes. Then we drank beer, shot the breeze with other long-beards. They were mostly fishermen: Swedes, Norwegians, Finns – basically, Scandinavians. From time to time, there were German and Dutch yachtsmen – fellows that seemed desperate and incomprehensible to me. On most nights, the crowd at the pub was large. It was a big, dark space, smoky and sooty. The long bar, the owner always at the counter, a bearded, good-natured loudmouth Viking. Everybody smoked pipes, cheap cigars or cigarettes. There was lots of smoke. They talked loudly, laughed loudly, loudly knocked their beer mugs and loudly moved their chairs. They did everything loudly... Each night, around ten o'clock, four musicians would go up to a small stage. One played an accordion or harmonica, another a guitar, the third was a drummer and the fourth would sit in front of a small black piano, playing and singing. Old microphones gave off an extraordinary sound. The musicians played songs from pre-war movies... From "Sun Valley Serenade" and other beloved films. But on that night, they weren't there. Somebody said that the pianist had fallen ill, and no performance was possible without him. There was no music that night, and because of that, one could hear the wind on the other side of the window; it whistled, reminding all of us that were on a small island, that it was cold out here, that we were surrounded by a dark sea, in which so many sailors have perished and many more are yet to perish... For some reason, without music it was the dead friends that we remembered or those who were very far away. And She was so far away that I couldn't stand the absence of music. I simply had no strength...

That's when I walked up to the owner, and we exchanged a few words. He nodded and called his son, who was his twin, only smaller and not yet gray. The guy turned on the speaker system for me, checked the mic, which got everybody's attention, and nodded to me, as in, everything's O.K. I approached the piano, opened the lid, ran my fingers across the keys while standing, sat at the instrument... and began to play and sing. I sang without words... either sang or whistled. I played a song that everyone knew back in our country, but not here. There was no need for words. I sang without words and whistled... sometimes. Then the limping drummer came onstage, sat at the drums and started to play with great passion. Then the other two musicians appeared; they, as it turned out, had been there all along, drinking with their friends. The sounds of trumpet and accordion rose up. The musicians didn't know my song, but played wonderfully. The noise in the pub hushed. Everybody was listening, many were crying...

The young Swedes finished their song, and I finished my whiskey. It all lasted some six-seven minutes – a wondrous effect of music and alcohol! I was very impressed. I didn't expect such a strong and tender wave of feeling from these two skinny Northern youths. Everything that the words "I am so in love" describe once again came crashing down upon me. I backed away to the bar. I needed a little more whiskey.

21

In my shirt, neckerchief and jacket I looked either like a dubious spy or a bank clerk on a picnic. I really wanted to take off the jacket, but my shirt was stained… I got more whiskey… and spent another half hour listening to the concert without leaving the bar. The Swedes played a couple of excellent things and five very decent dance compositions. The crowd was dancing. But the impressions I got from that song I enjoyed so much only intensified my exhaustion. The alcohol kicked it and made me feel… like getting something to eat. There, on that small island, in the pub, they served such wonderful fish soup with smoked salmon and potatoes…! "I am hungry!" Declared my brain. "I'll eat something and go home." I answered and went downstairs to look for Max. Walking down those steps, I realized that I was a little drunk after all, but not too drunk. My head was clear, so was my heart, everything else felt like something between ease and abandon. "Then what part of me is tired?" I asked myself. "The soul, your excellency! The soul!" Came the response.

At first, I heard noises, then saw Max. He and four other guys our age tightly clustered next to the bar with their heads cocked, peering at the TV. It was showing boxing, two black men battling each other, both boxers glistening with sweat, while Max was, again, completely unbuttoned: jacket unbuttoned, the shirt unbuttoned midway to his chest. He has turned red and was noticeably drunk. His four buddies were properly drunk, too.

"Sanya!" Max roared, seeing me. "You and I are winning!" He pulled away from his company and came up to me. "That one is ours," he pointed at the screen. "The big one. He is winning! I bet on him. And they all bet the other one…"

I couldn't really tell who Max bet on, both boxers were quite big, but it was important to find out exactly what he was betting.

"Max! What did you bet? And who are these friends of yours?"

"Shhh!" Max pressed a finger to his lips. "They're nice guys. Came from Krasnodar. Quiet, Sanya! I bet my beard!"

I must have raised my eyebrows way too high, because Max quickly whispered in my ear:

"I told them that I've been wearing this beard for ten years, that nothing is dearer to me, but if our guy loses, I'm shaving it off, and if he wins, they're paying for us, the whole way. They agreed, because I told them that I'd shave it off right here, in the bathroom."

I looked at Max with distrust, then at the guys from the south, then at Max again, and realized that I too am rooting for the boxer… and not the one that Max had bet on.

I walked up to the guys from Krasnodar, met all of them and immediately forgot their names. I tried to watch the boxing match, but I couldn't. It was the seventh round and everything was somehow happening too sluggishly. I was either not drunk enough, or too much in love.

There were beer mugs and trays with chips and nuts on the bar counter. That's what Max and company drank and ate. I attached myself to a plate of chips. My God, to eat nothing all day, then find yourself in a place where you can order all kinds of food, and instead you start crunching on chips! But they were delicious. "Eating is actually delicious!" I thought, and realized that I would like some beer.

I understood that I shouldn't do this. No way should I do this. I will feel awful, it's wrong and wasteful… In the morning, my face will be revolting… I'll be ashamed to look at it, especially as I needed to have a good face and clean voice in the morning.

But the next second I decided that I really wanted to drink, that a small beer was nothing, nothing more than quenching my thirst and that, most importantly, I wasn't drunk yet and in control of the situation. So I ordered a small beer and finished it at once. A minute after I finished my beer, the boxer Max bet on knocked down his opponent. Max wanted to toast the occasion, but my beer was already gone… And so, very quickly, a fresh mug of beer was shoved into my hand, a big one this time… And I started to drink it.

"Sanya, don't worry!" Max sat on the bar stool next to me and hugged me by the shoulders. "Why are you so sour? Tomorrow, I mean today, everything will be fine! Don't be so sad. What is it, you don't like these guys? Forget about them. They're nice guys. They sold or maybe bought something successfully. Sure, they're assholes. But good, fun-loving guys."

"I'm not drinking anymore!" I said adamantly.

"Of course not! You're not supposed to! You've got to look after me. But I'll drink some more!"

"I hope your boxer loses already!" I declared and realized, by the way I said it, that I'd definitely had enough.

"Why is that? Sanya, that's not..."

"Max, I can't stand seeing your beard anymore!"

"I know that! But let that be the saddest thing in life! You know what the saddest sport in the world is?"

"In what way?"

"You know, the saddest sport, in every way!"

"The saddest for who? For the athletes or the spectators?"

"For everybody! For both!"

"Bobsled."

"What are you talking about? Bobsled is fun!"

"Then long-distance walking."

"You don't know what you're talking about! They've got big crowds walking those things, that's first of all! Secondly, they walk from point A to point B, which means there is some kind of movement across space, a road, a route, purpose. The spectators like it too. They've got athletes passing them, they get to see them for only two minutes and that's it. No! Pick a different sport! Think."

"I don't know, leave me alone, Max!"

"The saddest sport... is women's single figure skating! No matter how long this young and beautiful woman skates around the rink, no matter how eccentrically she stretches her arms forward or bends or twirls... no one will ever jump out to join her, to hug her! And so, she is left there alone, on ice. See! Sad, and also symbolic!"

"You come up with that yourself?" I asked Max.

"No, I heard it on the radio. Sanya! Come on, who else could dream up such nonsense? Of course, I've came up with it myself. Just thought of it to make you laugh. Not bad, right?"

"Super! Of course, women's single figure skating. She is trying so hard, so young and beautiful – all in vain! Exactly! Men's single figure skating, on the other hand – not cheerful, but still not so hopeless. For starters, you don't feel as bad for a man, secondly, it's already in some way part of a man's nature to be alone, and thirdly, it's absolutely..."

"Sanya, stop it! It's impossible talking to you. I was just joking. Joking! And you're all worked up again! Instead, think up about what a spectacle men's pair figure skating would be! I wonder, would they perform in identical costumes or different ones…"

At this moment, the guys from Karsnodar started to roar. Actually, they turned out to be pretty decent guys, just swearing a bit too much, otherwise…

Max's boxer fell and didn't get up. The guys from Krasnodar roared, the people on TV raved, Max flailed his hands while I sat there and smiled silently.

"Sanya! Did you see my briefcase?"

"What do you need it for?"

"My razor is in there…"

"You checked it in with your coat."

"Right!" Max said and went toward the coat check.

His face showed such misery. I came up to the guys who watched as he walked off.

"Guys! What are you doing? For him, this beard is… like I don't know what! Every day he grooms and clips it! Now what is he going to do with all his little combs and scissors? You have to stop him! Let me pay for everything, just leave his beard. Go after him!"

The guys were at a loss.

"Well, we told him, you know, don't do it," said the thickest and sweatiest. "But he said, no, not a chance. Good for him!"

"We feel bad about it too! But a bet is a fucking bet! Are we men or what?" Another one said.

"Your Max, he is the man! And we'll pay for everything, it's no problem!" Said the third one.

"Definitely assholes," I thought, "but nice guys. Max was right, as always. So let them pay."

22

Max returned in roughly ten minutes. Good thing he was back, because I couldn't take any more of these Krasnodarovites with their southern accent and nonstop discussion of every woman that either appeared on television or happened to be around the club, including waitresses and managers. The discussion focused on their endowments, along with bold suppositions about how this one or that one might prefer it… and what's the best thing to do with one versus another…

Max came back frowning and with a droopy look. He was terribly changed. Turns out he had gotten used to his beard. He cut himself in several places, to which he applied little pieces of toilet paper. Max's face turned red and conveyed intense sorrow. Except I could tell that he was red from fighting back an irrepressible urge to explode in laughter. But Max held strong!

At once, they poured him a drink, slapped his shoulder, both of them to be exact, told him that he was the man and a good sport… I looked at Max without his beard and… I suddenly remembered. I remembered how I could've known that tall man who sat at the little table and later met my gaze… back there… in the café on the Avenue of Peace.

He was the same man who was with Her, back in the summer, at the housewarming… Except back then he had a beard. And now, the beard was gone… Everything became clear… Not everything, but many things…! And if not clear, then evident… And I was now free of doubts that he was the one sitting at the wheel of the Mercedes and waiting… Sure, many other questions were gnawing at me, but at this point they were minor, contemplative questions…

I got the urge to call Her right away and confess everything, ask everything, to warn Her. But it was already late and I was drunk. That it was late – that was hardly a problem, not as serious as the later circumstance. Calling while drunk wasn't an option! But to go and question this Mercedes figure – that I could do. All I had to do was talk it over with Max. Wouldn't do it without him. This type of business was impossible without Max...

I waited until we were done "celebrating" the passing of Max's beard. I declined to drink myself. The guys empathized with Max, and he played his role magnificently. Then I took him to the side and off to the coat check. Max was, for lack of a better word, smashed. He was holding up, but swaying lightly from side to side.

"You know, Sanya, I think I'm pretty smashed," he said.

It was a good sign. A rare one, too! Typically, Max wouldn't admit a thing like that. More often than not, he would get drunk, gush for a little while, meaning dance, declaim toasts, conceive some daring schemes, and then poof... down and asleep in some corner or gone without trace. At times like that, trying to convince him that he shouldn't drink any more was completely futile. But suddenly he admits it himself!

"Sanya, you didn't look after me! You didn't take care of me at all! And I, by the way, I listen to your every word! And obey everything!" He puffed out his shaved chin. "Sanya, let's get out of here. I want to eat. Let's go... Let me just..."

He went off to the restroom.

A bouncer came up to me.

"Here, your friend left this in the bathroom," he pointed with his eyes at the sauntering Max and his finger at the briefcase. It was up on a shelf at the coat check.

The bouncer said this with a smile, without vexation or anger. Clearly, Max had a chance to make him laugh as well and make an impression... The briefcase looked as though it had been jumped on and kicked repeatedly. Maybe that's exactly what happened... I picked up the briefcase... and went to the restroom to fetch Max.

Max was washing up. He splashed himself all ever, sniffing and huffing, bending under the tap to wet his head and then wagging it like a dog. After shutting off the water, he rolled off about a hundred meters of toilet paper and began drying himself. I waited for the end to these procedures and gave him back the briefcase. He took it. He did it mechanically, like it was something self-evident, without saying thank you, just took the briefcase and walked out of the restroom all disheveled.

I stood by the urinal and sensed that I was pretty drunk myself. I only realized this when performing actions that required a certain precision. I was drunk. "It's all that beer!" I thought to myself. Then I washed up a little and looked at myself in the mirror. The eyes and lips betrayed a considerable degree of intoxication. I looked at myself and disagreed with what I saw.

After I left the restroom, I saw Max waiting for me… He was fresh, groomed and excited. A little pale perhaps, but all in all he looked fabulous.

"You're as bright as a Phoenix, aren't you!" I said with admiration

"Don't put me down like that! I am much brighter! What about you? Looking a bit deflated, Sanya."

"I am deflating, Max, let me go. I have to get some sleep," I started moaning.

"Alright, sure. But let's stop by somewhere to get something to eat. I am really hungry. Just not to a place with too many women, or I'll be distracted. And also… make sure they've got normal food there. I mean… you know… meat!"

"My God! Where can I possibly take you? Max, it's not healthy to eat meat before bedtime! You'll have nightmares…"

"Excellent! I love horror movies, though I haven't been to the movies in a while."

Arguing or dissuading him were both pointless. I remembered a small American restaurant on October Square. A tiny American cabin with food. I have never been to America, but it seemed like in all the American movies the heroes either ate or just sat in such tiny cabins. Twenty-four hours a day, you could get a half-a-bucket-size portion of salad, a mountain of potatoes and an epic piece of meat. Just meat. They cooked fast, there was no dancing, the way it ought to be.

"Let's go!" I said

"Let's go!" Said Max. "But let's drive through the center, to air out a little."

I nodded. Max went over to the door, separating the foyer from the main hall, where his new buddies were still hanging out. He waved to them, shouted something and came back to me. His briefcase was with him.

"Nice guys," he said on our way out, "excellent really! Too bad they're assholes."

23

We left the club. Taxis lined the curbside. Lots of them. Right away, drivers rushed over to us with offers to "get us there at a good price". I scanned for the Mercedes. It was there. Max was about to come up to a random taxi when I stopped him and told him about my theory. I had to tell him the whole back story, not that it was particularly long. Max stopped to think.

"See that, Sanya, I was right! A jealous one! He'll be following us around till he finds out where you sleep."

"That part I get, but why did he wait by my building last night?" I asked.

"You're such a fool, Sanya. I don't understand, how is it that you're still living in Moscow…? He's lost her, that's all. Tried to find her, figured she might be with you. Besides, we can only guess what's going on there between them. That shouldn't concern you. If this guy is so distraught, enough to pitifully chase after you all over Moscow, then you've got the upper hand. Don't worry. I'm telling you, we'll sort it out."

"Let's go up right now and take the pressure off."

"Sanya, look at yourself right now. You're drunk! You're going to go and square off with a sober, tired, hungry, miserable man? I'll say it again, he's got it worse than we do. If you feel bad for him, go ahead, sort it out."

I understood. Everything that Max was saying was pure truth. I felt better. I even felt pity for this older and clearly desperate man. I recalled the way he sat at the table in the café and peered at something in front of him with an unseeing gaze. He must've bumped into me there by accident. When he saw me, his face changed so much! Poor guy! Back in the summer, I even gave him my business card. It must be hard for him. It probably has been for a long time. And who, I wondered, was the guy who picked Her up after the opening of the salon? Maybe the fellow in the Mercedes is also spying on him? And what if that other guy starts following me too? Who is he exactly? Who is he to Her? And what about this one, in the Mercedes?

Still, my thinking about this was sufficiently calm. I realized that I wasn't troubled by Her men. That She had them before or had them still... How many... I have always been very jealous. Especially after relationships ended and infatuations passed – but jealousy, it always lingered: how could someone else be allowed to take my place? But there was no jealousy now. There was just unbearable love. And the thought: "As long as she is happy! Of course, I'd prefer that she would be with me! But if it's not with me...? Let her be happy, that's all!" But for some reason I believed that I was now her number one. And that put me at ease.

Max and I got into the taxi of the busiest-looking driver. He showed the greatest tenacity and, more than anyone, was bumping his own rate. We didn't like him, but still got into his car. He was simply too active.

I told him where to go. Max asked him to drive us across the center. Getting in the car, he said: "I am feeling kind of tired, Sanya." He said it so sadly and so... believably! That tone did not at all correspond to his recent cheer. Max sat next to the driver, I sat in the back. We drove off in silence. Meaning that Max and I were silent, but the driver talked.

"We shouldn't be driving through the center. The road is bad. Too much snow. It'll take a long time. My tires, completely bald." The driver complained. "Can't put on winter tires, you know how much new rubber costs. And the gas..."

"Stop moaning! You keep moaning, we'll get out and not pay. Got it?" Max said very firmly. "And what do you mean you're driving us on naked rubber? You want to kill us? Just cost you ten percent!"

"Guys! That's not what I mean..."

"Be quiet, will you!" Max cut him off. "You're the driver, so drive! You keep running your mouth and we'll get out. I don't feel like listening to you. You think my life is easy? All I need is your whining!"

Max spoke so harshly that even I felt uneasy. His words and tone conveyed the unmistakable rigidity, simplicity and harshness of remote industrial cities and towns. But this rigidity was fair. I was also disgusted listening to the taxi driver's complaints. He whined hoping for some miserly extra cash. Idiot. He couldn't understand that when somebody is whining and pleading, the mere thought of giving that person money makes you sick.

The driver shut up and we drove in silence. Max pressed his head against the glass and looked outside. I leaned back and closed my eyes...

No, this time I did not end up in a trench or on the bridge of a ship. I closed my eyes, reclined on the back seat, and the darkness which formed in my brain from closing my eyes... this darkness began to spin, slowly at first, then faster and faster. "The helicopters!" I told myself. "For you are drunk off your ass, your excellency," a sober and powerful voice boomed. It came from the part of me that did not control movement, facial expressions or the accuracy of word pronunciation. It came from the place where I watched my drunk self and mused about it.

Helicopters! They find a drunk person even in the most secluded of places, even in complete silence and bliss of some heavenly corner, they penetrate the most defended and concealed private property. You cannot hide from them.

You can escape from your friends at some banquet. Escape, feeling full of strength, and think that this time you managed not to drink too much, that a few glasses of champagne, followed by cognac – a lot of it, but good cognac! – it's no big deal... Escape from everyone, rush to the taxi and hurry to the one who is waiting for you... But the moment you lean back on your seat and close your eyes, the helicopters catch up to you. An entire squadron of them overtakes your taxi, hangs over it and spins you, the car and the whole city... And after that, there is no more need for anybody, wherever they may be, to wait up for you.

Or you might get some beer with friends in springtime. The evening is so warm, with lilacs, aromas and boulevards! Then off to have dinner at some restaurant, drink some vodka. Then hang out a little more and drink beer. Then get together with her and drink whatever she is drinking, which means something sweet and syrupy, walk her home, kiss her good night, take your jacket off her shoulders and take a stroll down the boulevard, then sit on a bench and enjoy a cigarette. But as you sit down to relax, as soon as you take that first drag and, closing your eyes to exhale smoke, as if bursting from the bushes of lilac, come the helicopters and the bench starts twisting up from the ground counterclockwise like a corkscrew...

Or you come home a little drunk and tired after talking... and more talking. It's quiet at home, clean and cool. Summertime! Curtains fluttering by the open balcony door. You commend yourself for not bringing anyone home... Think you'll wash up tomorrow, that tomorrow you'll take a shower, but right now you must go to sleep. So you toss your clothes right on the floor and collapse into that cool and fresh bed... But the moment the back of your head touches the pillow, they fly in – into the room, across the balcony door, thought the window, tearing down the curtains – the helicopters.

If you open your eyes, it doesn't get any better... Not anymore! You can hardly keep them open long enough... and the helicopters zero in for a new raid... Which means that what awaits you in the morning is suffering and being alone in that suffering.

"That Benz right there, it's driving behind us the whole time," I heard the driver's voice.

"Yes, it is," said Max, "and it will be. You know what's in here?" Max pointed to his briefcase. "That's right! We had five of them following us, we lost the rest, but can't shake this one. Go ahead! If you lose him, I'll pay you double."

"Oh, come on!" The driver answered. "Stop pulling my chain! But it is definitely driving after us all the way from the club."

"That's what I'm trying to tell you!" Max went on. "So are we going to lose him or what?"

"How can we lose him?! It's a Merc. There isn't enough road either," the driver whined. "But I guess I could try..."

"Don't," I said.

By then we were driving past the Kremlin across The Great Stone Bridge.

"Let's get off to the embankment," I said in a weak voice.

"Look how much time I'd already lost with you," the driver nearly sobbed.

"Fine! Keep driving, you'll be washing it all off yourself." I announced.

"Sanya, are you sick?" Max turned to face me. "Pull the fuck over! What're you moaning all the time for?" He said to the driver in disgust. "We'll pay you, don't piss your pants..."

We turned right off the bridge, then went under it, came out to the embankment and stopped across from the Kremlin. I quickly came out of the car, crossed the roadway and walked right up to the river.

"Don't piss your pants, we won't leave you. Just sit tight and wait. Some man you are," I heard Max's voice behind me. The snow crunched nearby. Max walked behind me.

"Sanya, do it old-school! Two fingers down your throat…"

"Wait, Max, wait."

"Ok, I'll shut up."

We were standing on fresh snow. A frozen river lay before us, and farther ahead, beautifully lit, rose the Kremlin. The snow covered the battlements of the wall along with the slopes and ledges of the towers. And soaring above it all, like outlandish air balloons, were the domes of the cathedral…

It was cold. Behind, cars passed from time to time. We stood in silence.

"You're right," Max said. "It's not right to barf here."

I stood in silence and thought nothing. I was breathing. Breathing in cold air…

"Yes. You know, Sanya, we're already used to this view. Postcards, posters, TV. From childhood – the Kremlin, the Kremlin! And here it is! Imagine how amazing it must be for some Japanese or Australian to see it. Sanya, maybe I'm stupid, but I find it very strange." He gestured at the Kremlin widely. "Isn't it strange? It doesn't look like anything. Right, Sanya?"

"You're right, Max, this is some very strange shit!" I said and nodded.

Once, I remember standing on the Red Square early in the morning. There weren't many people. I was looking at the Kremlin and thinking, there it is, the Kremlin. And I am seeing it not on a television screen back in my hometown and not on some old New Year's greeting card, but right here. I can come right up to it, even touch it. And now I'm living in Moscow, a mere ten kilometers away from the Kremlin, and yet none of this helps me get closer to it. It is equally distant from me… whether I'm standing in front of it on the Red Square or seeing it on TV, as far away from it as, say, Vladivostok. For me, what's happening there, behind those walls, is just as incomprehensible and remote! This distance cannot be measured in units of length. It's simply insurmountable! Therefore, it doesn't matter if I am in Moscow or Khabarovsk… The Kremlin remains just as far away and magical as it was in childhood.

But now I was at ease. I was looking at this strange and, in every sense of the word, wondrous, how should I put it, this strange thing – the Kremlin, and it put me at ease.

Lately, I haven't really been watching the news. Didn't watch TV at all. Before, I didn't just love the news, I couldn't live without it. Every morning I'd watch several news programs on different channels. I compared how different channels reported the same facts. It was terribly important for me to know what moves were being made inside the government, how the fight against corruption was going, the consequences of the typhoon that struck Sakhalin, what was new in aviation design, as well as ecology, sports, weather. I was interested in everything.

But now it was clear that nothing interesting or, more precisely, significant was happening. Anywhere! Neither out in the world not behind these walls. Nothing significant. Why watch the news when all they show are unattractive faces, saying things which are mostly untrue? They might also show some cow-breeding farm and, if nothing else, forest fires somewhere in Canada. Except they've got plenty of forests there, and, secondly, they know how to put out fires. So why watch it? It's obvious, is it not, that everything that's happening now is happening only to me. The rest of the world can take a break... I am at the center now... Better yet, the center – is me. Sure, there was a plane crash in Pakistan! But I was the one driving to the airport. The interplay of such events is often not so easy to establish...

A car honked behind us. It was our taxi driver pressing on the horn. Rushing us.

"I think I'm just going to beat him up now," said Max. "How did we end up with this kind of scum?" And, raising his voice, he shouted to the driver: "Beep one more time, and I'll make you retake the road test! Got it? A paid test!" Max lowered his voice. "What a piece a trash! Speaking of which, there is yours." Max pointed at the Mercedes, which was now parked just up the street.

"Alright, let's hit the road," I said.

"You good?"

"Fine, let's go."

"Wait, Sanya, I am sorry. I know this is very provocative and symbolic, but I can't hold it anymore," Max said and unbuttoned his fly.

We were peeing on the snow, facing the Kremlin. Peeing without pathos or protest. I left a single deep cavity in the snow, Max carved out some intricate monogram.

24

We drove out to Yakimanka and picked up speed. There weren't many cars, everybody drove fast. Once outside the center, people saw the wide and open road before them and pressed on the gas. Nice new cars passed us from both sides and flew ahead. Smoke from the tailpipes, mixing with whirlwinds of snow, rose from the roadway.

"Sure! They've got crazy power under those hoods!" Said the driver.

"What do you care? You've got bald tires! Drive carefully," said Max.

We were quickly approaching October Square when an Audi, rudely cutting in front of us from the right, attempted another brazen maneuver to overtake the next car up ahead. The car in front of us wriggled slightly to the right. After that, I could no longer understand what was happening, but that car, the one that wriggled... went sliding sideways, tipped an old Volvo in the right lane and, like a bullet, flew farther askew... The driver must have slammed on the breaks, but the road was too slippery. The ill-fated car barreled out of the roadway, knocked down the billboard stand... The Volvo must have hit the brake too – the car spun out and, in the next instant, smashed into a large Jeep. Our driver cut sharply to the left, our car skidding and sliding toward the wreck... Two seconds before it happened, it became clear that the impact was inevitable. The headlights were fast approaching, our driver doing everything he could...

"Hold on!" Max shouted.

We barely tipped, but the hit was so powerful that it spun us one hundred and eighty degrees and flipped the car on the side. I dropped to the bottom, Max fell on top of the driver, everything froze...

Cold air rushed inside the taxi. The windshield was completely blown out... We were lying on the left side...

"You alive?" Max shook the driver. "Sanya, how about you?"

We were all in one piece. Seconds later, we crawled out of the taxi. The car that crashed into us was some distance away, running from it toward us, a stout looking fellow was shouting: "Thank God! Guys, thank God!" Others ran to us from other directions.

Max darted across the street to the collided Volvo and Jeep. The grey Audi was nowhere in sight.

"The fucker ran away!" Our diver said, rubbing his shoulder.

I ran after Max. My left knee hurt a little bit. Otherwise, I was fine. I thought I hit my face against the front seat, but couldn't feel anything yet...

The Volvo took a terrible hit to the right side. It was frightening to look at. Another few seconds passed. People, maybe five of them, who ran to other collided cars, momentarily froze once there, as if not daring to touch somebody else's tragedy. Max jumped up to the Volvo and tore open the back door. It opened instantly. There were intermittent cries of a woman. Meanwhile, Max was trying to open the driver door. He opened it, but not right away.

"Why are you standing around like sheep?!" Max roared. "At least call somebody!"

A police car was already speeding toward us along the middle lane. It wailed its siren and flashed its lights.

Max finally managed to open the door... From there, a young man in a blue jacket fell into his arms. At once, everything became animated again and everyone started screaming at the same time. Somebody opened the driver door of the Jeep. The Jeep wasn't damaged at all. Inside was a small woman in a little fur coat, holding her head with both hands. There were glasses on her sharp face. She closed her eyes.

"Sanya, check on that, will you," Max shouted and pointed in the direction of the standalone car that crashed into the billboard.

Strangely enough, there was practically nobody around it. Two people were fumbling with the doors. I ran up to them. The car was some old, two-door thing, a Japanese one... The doors were completely jammed. There was some commotion inside. Behind the wheel was a man of about forty. He hit his head on the windshield. He got it pretty bad. His face was badly broken and he had damaged the steering wheel with his chest. The woman on the passenger seat behaved very well: she was crying, but not panicking.

EVGENY GRISHKOVETS

The doors wouldn't budge. The windows didn't lower. The man at the wheel was obviously trapped.

"Cover your face, we're about to break the windshield," shouted a tall man in a long dark coat, signaling with his hands for clarity. He'd run up to us a few moments earlier. It was the same man from the café… I took quick glance around. The Mercedes was parked about fifteen meters further down the road… Its door was ajar, so was its trunk… In his hand, my pursuer held some kid of metal object, a car jack, I thought. We were doing everything very quickly.

"Hang on!" I yelled out and, for some reason, I don't know why, instantly shed my coat, grabbed the metal piece, wrapped it in my coat and struck it against the windshield.

Everything was happening so quickly…

We extracted the woman rather easily. She was stout. She was nearly unscathed, except for what looked like a broken right arm and a badly dislocated shoulder. She had been buckled, but the man had not.

We laid her down on the snow. At first, I dropped my coat on the snow, then we put her over it. She was very worried about her husband. But we couldn't pull him out by ourselves. He had lost consciousness and was rasping loudly; when we were busy with him, I accidently touched his chest, stained myself with blood and felt that his ribcage was broken. I could tell that it was broken completely.

That's when several ambulances came rushing at the same time. People in vests scattered. We were immediately dismissed, pushed aside. I walked off… I remembered the feeling of touching the beaten, broken body. I felt sick… All sounds quieted. Everything that was happening around me started to resemble the ending of an American movie, when the road is jammed up with different flashing cars.

I walked off to the side and, under my shirt, felt cold sweat on my back. I hunched over and vomited. My stomach was practically empty, nothing but liquid. I folded over one more time, then took a few steps, fell to my knees and fainted.

The train car was swaying gently, wheels knocking; the compartment was dark. I sat with my eyes closed, but wasn't asleep. My compartment neighbor, a marine captain, a very thin and not talkative man, was lying on the top bunk moaning loudly in his sleep. On the bottom bunk, across from mine, slept an artillery major. He was snorting. I never learned to sleep while somebody is snoring. I could fall asleep with people talking, singing, laughing all around. With dogs barking, cows mooing, birds singing – I could sleep. But if someone snored, even in the next room – I woke up and couldn't fall back asleep. I woke up even from my own snoring…

I sat in the train car, our echelon pushing ahead… and I was tired. Tired! I was tired of talking myself down, of telling myself that everything was going to be alright, or that it was alright already. Tired of coaxing myself to be steady, kind… stable. Tired of telling myself: "Wait, we'll sort it out!" Wait for what? Sort what out? Everything has already been decided.

I sat there and quietly wept… wept to myself…

A terrific explosion tackled the train car, blew out the windows, a flash of light outside the window lit everything red. Another explosion…! The train kept moving. Horrifically loud sounds came from everywhere. Explosions, cries, the knocking of the train, the howling of diving airplanes. We were under bombardment…

I was the first to run out into the corridor, the marine captain following. People were running out of the compartments… most of the windows had shattered…

"Feet! Watch your feet! Glass!" Somebody shouted.

At that moment, the lights went on inside the train car.

"Kill the fucking lights!" I cried out. "Kill the light! They can see us…"

I was less afraid of us being visible from the airplanes than I was of somebody seeing me cry…

25

When I regained consciousness, I was sitting on the back seat of a car. The door was open and I was sitting sideways, my legs outside, with the rest of me inside. My coat was tossed over my shoulders. I was sitting inside the Mercedes. Max and the man in the long coat stood nearby, talking. The man was smoking. A siren wailed and one of the ambulances sped away. The crowd had thinned out. Even some journalists had driven up with their cameras.

"Sanya! How are you?" Asked Max.

"Alive," I answered.

I spoke and felt that my lips were swollen and my jaw in pain. But there was no blood on my face.

"Your guy has been taken away. Hope he makes it. The woman has been taken away too, in another car. But she was alright," Max told me.

"You didn't happen to memorize the plate number of the car that fled?" Asked the owner of the Mercedes.

"No, I didn't notice. Grey Audi… and that's it," I replied.

"Isn't that something, nobody got a good look at him!" Said Max. "He is less than human… The guy in the Volvo, totally mangled, they had to cut him out of the car, couldn't get to him otherwise. The driver is alive, two girls on the back seat, one without a scratch, but the other, her legs, a shredded mess. A nightmare, pure nightmare. Imagine that hit! Heavy Jeep…"

"Yes, it was a horrible impact, I was actually driving right behind the Jeep," said the man in a coat, "barely swerved away. The lady hit the brake, but what's the use! It's not even her fault…"

"By the way, I'm Max," Max introduced himself and stretched out his hand.

"Mikhail Alekseevi… Oh, just Mikhail," said our pursuer and shook Max's hand.

"And this is Sasha," Max said referring to me.

I nodded.

"I know," said Mikhail.

"Listen, why have you been following us all the time?" Max asked in his inimitable voice.

"That is something I am not going to discuss with you."

"Still, it's kind of strange, you know, the whole day…" said Max with a certain provocation.

"Stop! I told you, I am not going to talk about this," this was said sharply and decisively.

Just then, the fellow who drove the car that collided with out taxi ran up to us.

"Guys! I am so glad you're alive, my God!" he was smiling. He was holding a bottle in his hand. A beautiful bottle. "My driver couldn't swerve away. What a nightmare! My wife still can't speak. And today was my birthday! An anniversary! Just passed into my seventh decade, imagine that. We get ready to head home, and now this…"

"Happy Birthday," Max said and shook his hand. "And what about you… everybody alright?"

"Knock on wood! If we crashed head on… that'd be it, guys, we wouldn't be talking right now… Mine is almost a tank. Look at yours though, you barely tipped over and look how you spun out. It was liked in a movie."

"Yes! True, like in a movie," Mikhail nodded his head.

"Here, guys, take it," he handed us the bottle. "They keep giving them to me, except I don't drink!" He smiled crookedly, as if to apologize for not drinking. "I am old enough to have had my share."

Out of politeness, Max refused it a couple of times, but eventually took the bottle.

"Drink to good fortune and to the one up there," he pointed his finger up to the sky. "Who is still watching over us. And if it isn't too ghastly for you, drink one to me. It's my birthday after all!"

"Who are we drinking to?" Asked Max

"Ah, yes!" He took a few business cards out of his pocket and gave one to each of us. "If I can ever be of service – don't hesitate. When you call, say you're my nocturnal friends from Yakiman-ka, and I'll remember. Bye guys! My car is ready, we're off. Good luck!"

We said goodbye, he jogged back to the car where a tall large man stood waiting for him. A bodyguard or driver, or both…

"Nice fellow," said Max. "'The Government of Russia,'" he read the business card. "'Deputy Minister'..." Max whistled and shoved the card inside his pocket.

Another ambulance approached with a howl.

"I'll go check on our racer before they slap handcuffs on him," Max said. "Mikhail, could you wait a bit, let Sasha sit here a bit longer, I'll be quick."

"Of course I'll wait, where would I go without you?" Said Mikhail with a bitter smirk.

"Thank you," said Max, shoved the bottle in my hands and ran off.

"Take your briefcase," I called after him weakly.

Then came the quiet. Sure, there was noise all around, but all I sensed was the quiet, or silence, to be exact. Mikhail lit up a cigarette. I looked around inside his car. It was clean, there were newspapers on the back seat along with a large bottle of mineral water. The man has spent the entire day in his car and managed not to trash it, didn't pile it with cigarette butts and ash...

We were silent.

It was as though all air and strength have been pumped out of me. I sat there feeling nothing at all, except emptiness. "If only I could call Her," something said inside my head. I wanted to call Her, I also wanted to wash up with warm water and... have some soup. Thick hot soup.

We were silent...

I detected within myself some strange sense of guilt that I now experienced before this man, who stood there and smoked, before this tall and strong person who was considerably older than myself. I have always experienced something similar to that next to the people who weren't doing so well while I was riding high, or next to those who, frankly, had less money than I did. Mikhail was certainly worse off than I was. He stood there, smoking one cigarette after another, oblivious to the temperature of the surrounding air... while I was freezing. I had no scarf, I'd lost it somewhere, the coat was damp, wrinkled, and I had to put it back on... I had to put it on and button it up, but I had no strength. I started fixing the neckerchief around my neck and noticed that my hands were covered in blood. Somebody else's blood. The shirt was completely soiled... Nevertheless, I stood up, scooped up some snow, rubbed my hands. Then I put on my coat and sat back down.

We were silent.

I studied the bottle that Max shoved into my hands. Cognac. The name was unfamiliar to me, but it certainly contained lots of superfluous letters – the cognac must have been good. They don't give bad cognac to members of government on their sixtieth birthday… Mikhail kept smoking.

"That's it, we can get out of here," said Max as soon as he returned.

"He's got his briefcase," I thought.

"What about witness statements?" Asked Mikhail.

"They've got enough witnesses, I left our phone numbers. If you like – please, but Sanya and I are leaving," said Max and winked at Mikhail.

Mikhail didn't say anything. So Max continued:

"You know who memorized the plate number of the Audi? Our driver! Some guy he turned out to be! You hear that, Sanya? He remembered it! And he had the nerve to tell me that we didn't pay him. I gave him some money and he looks unhappy. I tell him: 'You didn't even get us to the destination, I can just not pay at all.' So he starts moaning, that his car is crashed and what's he going to do now. So I ask him: 'Are you saying I have to buy you a new car now?' And he tells me that he was driving us, and if hadn't been for us, he wouldn't have gone this way. Makes sense, right? But what a con man, this guy! Anyway, let's go. Is it far?"

"No, we're almost there," I replied.

"Some 'almost'!" Max smirked.

"It's walking distance, over there," I showed with my hand. "A five-minute walk."

"Get in, I'll take you, I'm following you anyway, so go ahead," said Mikhail, "get it."

"Thank you!" Said Max. "Very kind of you! Hear that, Sanya?"

"Yes, thank you!"

"Let's do away with the wise cracks!" Said Mikhail. "Just get in. Where to?"

"To that American restaurant, there. Do you know it...?" I said.

"I do," he answered. "God, what am I doing? This is madness! Madness!" He said quietly, but with desperation.

We drove in silence. As predicted, it was a two-minute drive. He drove up to the restaurant and stopped. We sat in the car, not getting out, not knowing what to do.

"Why don't you come in with us, have some coffee," Max said at last. "Otherwise, why sit here, it just seems…"

"No, I won't come. Don't ask me…"

"Come on, really," I said, "just come, it's awkward. If…"

"Please," he interrupted, "don't talk to me! I can't be talking to you. I am very tired and can lose it. Let's not make the situation any more foolish or absurd than it already is! Be quiet, please!"

"Fine," said Max. "But we're going to have some food, maybe you'd like a little…"

"Do what you want, forget about me, for God's sake."

"But, excuse me," I insisted. "how are we supposed forget it if you are following us all the time…"

"Shut up!" He screamed. "Enough! I drove you here, didn't I? That's it! Get out of my car! Go away!"

We got out at once. Max shrugged. He was holding his briefcase, I was holding a bottle. We walked towards the restaurant. The Mercedes remained in place.

26

"I am sorry, but you cannot bring your own alcohol in here," said a young woman, who was greeting guests at the door, "it's not allowed."

"But we're not going to…" I was about to explain, but Max interrupted.

"My dear, have you heard what happened over there, not far from here," Max motioned his hand indistinctly, "that there was a serious car accident just now?"

"Yes, one of our visitors mentioned something. Not long ago," the woman was very young. Max leaned closer to her and read what was written on her chest tag. She backed away slightly.

"Yelena," Max read aloud. "Lenochka! Can you imagine, we were actually victims of that accident. We've only been in Moscow since morning and now this! Awful stress! But what a city Moscow is, Lenochka! Are you from Moscow?"

"Yes."

"Native?"

"I was born here."

"There you go. See, lucky you! And we got into an accident as soon as we came here! But then came the police and the doctors and issued us this bottle. Said that we must absolutely drink it, that it will relieve stress and relax us… Sanya, how did they put it exactly? 'It will accelerate the post-traumatic recovery!' That's right! And how could we disobey policemen and doctors? We are guests of the Capital! Lenochka, just look what kind of excellent cognac they give out to accident victims in Moscow!"

"I'll ask the manager," said the girl, totally confounded.

"Lenochka! We'll show ourselves in, alright? We'll hide the bottle. We really are coming from the accident," I said. "We need to clean up and get something to eat. Alright?"

"Yes, yes, of course! Please go ahead, you'll be comfortable over here," she said in exactly the way she has been instructed to say it.

I took my time washing up with warm water. At first, I studied my face for a while. I got hit badly by the headrest of the front seat, though I couldn't remember it. The right cheekbone was swollen, so were my lips, the jaw moved, but not without pain. The hair... anyway, it was obvious I had to clean my head. Thank God I got that haircut – otherwise, it would've been too painful to look at. It was as though extra skin had formed upon my forehead, that's how deep the creases were. Bristles of hair were already sprouting from my face. How does the body produce all this? In fact, I remember, back in the army, how amused I was that the worse the conditions were, the more tense the days, the faster my beard and nails grew. Although, perhaps, it only seemed that way to me – time had simply flown by faster... Or maybe I was right, who knows...

I was scrubbing the remainder of blood off my hands. The water turned pink. "Like in a movie," I thought. That's how murderers wash someone else's blood off their hands. Come into a restaurant, go to the restroom and wash it off.

Curious, isn't it, how whenever something highly, or even slightly unusual happens, right away you think: "Like in a movie."

I just wanted to take off the shirt and throw it out. It was caked with stains, and over the course of the day I'd sweated through it, and dried it out at least ten times. The neckerchief twisted around my neck in a strange way and now looked more like a rope. I washed up and came back to the main hall of the restaurant. Max sat with his head in his hands, elbows resting firmly on the table. He closed his eyes. I could tell how tired he was...

"Go wash up, Max. You'll feel better. And then we'll go to my place. We have to get some sleep."

"Sure, sure. I'll go wash up now, sure," Max mumbled, opening his eyes, but he wouldn't get up. "Sanya, can you imagine, that guy, on the front seat... you know, the one in the Volvo... He died, probably instantly. His whole body shattered, but his face was unharmed, smooth. Eyes closed. Probably was so startled that he shut his eyes, and the expression on his face... Not even fear, but some kind of refusal, as in, 'I don't want to!'"

After those words, Max picked up the bottle that sat on the next chair. The bottle was open and the level of liquid inside already lower. Max took a good swig, squinted and stretched the bottle to me. I shook my head.

"The guy is a mess though," Max continued, flailing his hand toward the Mercedes parked outside. "A serious mess. God forbid! Terrible!"

"Max, that's not fair either. It's crazy, chasing people all over the city...! One needs to somehow, I don't know, keep it together..."

"Sanya, how the fuck would you know what he needs or doesn't need? Can you imagine what kind of hell he is in right now? To reach a point where you're like this? He is ashamed of himself! Can't you see that? And this one is a real man, not some weakling! Not one to go around fainting..."

"Weakling or not, the fact that he is chasing after me all day – that's hysterical, Max! Real men don't get all hysterical like this. I don't pity him. Staging this circus! Playing some weird detective... I don't pity him!"

"And me?"

"What about you?"

"Do you pity me, Sanya? Why do you think I came? No business in town, no real reason. You think I came here to get drunk and hang out? That's it, right? Just to get drunk and hang out, sure!" Max's faces somehow sagged and, because of that, the corners of his eye angled, making them look like the eyes of a dog. An old, sad, beaten bastard.

That's when the waitress brought us the menus. Right away, I asked for tea with lemon. There were still people at the restaurant. Not many. It was late at night.

"Sanya... my wife left me," Max said when the waitress walked away. He didn't finish the phrase when his chin began to tremble.

He said this and quickly brought the bottle back to his mouth. Twice Max gulped feverishly and coughed, sprinkling cognac on the table in front of him. Large tears appeared in his eyes. He began to cry, but without shuddering or sniffling. He cried only with his eyes.

"She left, Sanya... And you know something, she didn't leave me for somebody, but to get away from me. Understand? She left me! How am I going to live now? I can't stay there, back in our town. Everything is over for me. Everything!" Max was getting increasingly drunk. "Just don't think it's because I am ashamed to live there, that I'm afraid of gossip, that everybody will know that my wife left me. No, I'm not scared of that. It's not ever important! What's the difference now?" He took another sip. "Life is over, Sanya! I didn't have a wife! Before,

I didn't have one… Then I got married, and now she left! And now I have no wife again! And that's all! The circle has closed!"

We got our tea in a pot and two large cups. I said that we had yet to decide what we wanted to order. Before the waitress left, Max sat with his head turned away, peering into the dark window.

"Of course!" Max wiped his eye with his palm and made it into a fist, "I am a bastard. I know. Makes sense. I wasn't even surprised. She left so quietly, without fighting. We used to fight, but this time she left in a way that made it clear – that trying to stop her was pointless. I wanted to leave myself. Told her that I was leaving her. But she just smirked and left. And the way she looked at me, Sanya. That was it. She looked at me the way the doctor looked at that dead guy in the car. As if with regret, understanding and, you know… finality. Looked, saw everything and turned away. As though there was no more need to ask questions, like, how is he doing, doc?"

I poured some tea for Max and myself, tossed in slices of lemon, listened to Max and watched the tea brighten from citric acid.

"She left, Sanya, because there was nothing more to expect from me. No, really. Everything was clear. Even to me." Max took a loud slurp of the tea, burned himself, squinted, but went on. "I didn't love her that much. I didn't… But she loved me, Sanya. And that's that. I have always imagined that I could easily go on without her. You know… live without her. And you see? I can! But it's no longer the same life. I get it now, Sanya. I've now begun to live out the rest my life! Real life is over, and now comes the dying."

"Max, knock it off, stop piling it on."

"Sanya, piling it on or not, everything is simple. I had lived without her, then lived with her, and now again without her. And the living without her part – I've already been there. And if something repeats itself, it's not simply that it's unexciting, but it's no longer a life, Sanya! It isn't! It's living out the rest of it."

Max started drinking tea again. His drunken lips were disobedient, he loudly sucked in air with the tea and loudly exhaled after each sip. I started drinking mine too… I didn't know what to say, I had nothing to say. I just sat there, seeing what I saw, hearing what I heard, and that was all. At that moment, I lacked the strength to take part in the life that surrounded me. I knew that I had to simply sit and listen to my friend. And that there wasn't anything else I could do.

"Sanya, I often have this dream that I am being drafted back to the army. Really strange shit! As if the current me is drafted, boom, just like that… and I am being taken away. And in the dream I'm not even surprised, just thinking how to inform my wife, my parents. And then I think: when they bring me there, I should tell them that I'm not a newbie, that I've already, you know… served. I've always been so horrified by these dreams. I'd wake up and be so glad that I'm awake. But now I'd happily go back to the army. Any place… Sanya, when I was home by myself, I almost… Anyway, let me go wash up…"

He stood up, reached for the bottle, drank a little more while standing, put the bottle back on the table and went to the restroom.

"Get that off the table right now," I heard a sharp female voice. I raised my eyes and saw a young woman in a dark suit. "Or should I call security?"

"Forgive me. You're absolutely right, but the man is really unwell," I said quietly and slowly. "Our car nearly crashed, and somebody has just died, practically in my friend's arms. I'll get rid of the bottle. We won't do it anymore."

"It's just that you are displaying it so openly. Please, we've got cameras here. The management will be very unhappy," she said, softer this time.

"Of course! Thank you so much! Forgive us, we'll be leaving soon. Only could I have some soup? What kind do you have?"

"It's all on the menu, I'll send the waiter."

"I'm sorry, but I won't be able to read anything," I said in all honesty. "Please, just tell me."

"We have French onion soup, mushroom puree soup and borscht."

"Borscht? But this is an American restaurant?"

"It's an America restaurant in Russia!" She answered in a way that made it clear: she gets asked this question all the time.

"Borscht. Bring two, please. Do you honestly think that the management is watching what's happening, at this hour?"

The clock read 3:05. I was surprised, it felt like it was later.

"They watch the recordings," she smiled. "Everything is recorded."

"That must be quite a show! Great! Interesting people they are, your management."

"So, two servings of borscht?" She said, and smiled more cheerfully. "Anything to drink?"

"Cola, with ice and lemon. With lots of ice, please, and no need for a straw."

My phone rang. Its sound came as though from some hollow depth of my pocket. I thought that I'd already forgotten about this object. Phone! Where is it? I shoved my hand into the left pocket of my jacket and pricked myself on something sharp. I pulled out the cracked flashlight. I must have slumped on top of it back in the car, when we flipped over. There were shards still left in my pocket. I placed the flashlight on the table and brought the cut finger to my mouth. With my right hand, I pulled the phone out of the right pocket. It was Her!

27

The phone identified her number. It was Her calling!

28

I can neither define what I experienced nor convey the exact details of our conversation…

"Hello," I said and, for some reason, stood up.

She spoke in a tired, slightly cracked voice. There was so much warmth in that voice. She spoke rather quickly. She must have been preparing for the conversation.

She asked if she had woken me up, but then added that she probably didn't since she could hear music in the background.

"I am at a restaurant now," I answered. "Max and I are at a restaurant."

She asked if anything terrible happened to me.

And I, in turn, asked why she was asking.

She told me that she couldn't fall asleep after my call. And then, not long ago, felt such a strong sense of worry for me that she decided to call and find out what happened. She said she knew I would forgive her if she woke me.

I said that everything was fine, that all night I've been accompanying Max to different places all over Moscow. That we actually did, a short time ago, run into some hooligans, that I got hit in the face, but it was nothing serious, that everything turned out alright, which she'll see for herself next time we see each other.

She asked… quickly asked when we'd have that date. I said that I was ready any time, always…

She said, in a stirred and splendid way, that… she could come right away, if possible, or that I could come to her, that there was some twenty-four-hour place next to her house; she has never been there, but it seemed nice enough.

For about three seconds, I could say nothing.

So she continued. She said that after my call she only wanted one thing – to talk. Or rather, to speak. Not talk, but speak… And if it's no trouble, if at all possible… she wanted to do it right now.

While she talked, I looked at my shirt, touched my face with my left hand, turned my head and looked outside, towards a parking lot, where, under a street light, sat the Mercedes… I thought about Max, who was probably crying in the restroom at this very moment… I glanced at my shirt again…

I don't know how I mustered the words to say what I said next. I don't have the mind to explain it. I said that there was no way I could come over. That my friend Maxim was terribly drunk, that those hooligans, the ones I told her about, managed to take away his briefcase, which contained all the money and documents. I told her that I couldn't leave him right now, that we only came to a restaurant because Max was feeling sick and he was now in the bathroom. But that there was no reason to worry, and no need for her to come here herself. That I was getting ready to take Max home.

She was listening very, very quietly. Then she said that if he kept his money in a briefcase, there must have been a lot of it.

I said that, indeed, there was quite a lot of it.

Then, somehow, I managed to make a joke. She laughed quietly… without cheer.

She asked me to call her when I got home, that way she'd stop worrying. I promised that I would…

And that was that! Never in my life have I done anything more awful and treacherous. I sat back down and stared at the phone. Then picked up the bottle and, without hiding it, took a good swig…

EVGENY GRISHKOVETS

29

Max came back and sat down across from me. His hair was wet, he smoothed it to the side. His face was totally pale, he must've washed himself with cold water.

"Oh my! We've got collateral damage," said Max, looking at the broken flashlight. "Sanya, what's the matter now? You can't be left alone for even a minute. What happened? Don't worry about it so much! I know where they sell the same ones…"

I didn't respond at all, just sat there. I didn't know what to say or do. Good thing they brought the borscht.

"Borscht?" Max was surprised. "My goodness! Were you the one who ordered it? Brilliant! Turns out you're good for something and know a thing or two about life after all… Sanya, what's with you?"

I said nothing. I took a pepper shaker and sprinkled some into my borscht. I was doing it more out of habit rather than wishing to improve the taste… Max waited till I was done, took the shaker and did the same.

"What about sour cream?" He said loudly into some distance. "It doesn't work without sour cream, sweetheart!" He said to the girl who brought us the sour cream. "I realize that cognac with borscht is pretty obscene, but…"

He drank a little more cognac from the bottle, kneeling slightly so as not to make it look too obvious. Handed me the bottle. I took a sip… Squinted. Max waited for me.

We ate our borscht at the same time. It was hot, cooked well, the real thing, with a rich taste of garlic.

"I remember my grandmother always saying to me that borscht is good for your blood," Max was trying to pep me up. "And I'd always tried to eat more of it, thinking I need a lot of blood, the more the better."

The soft sound of old American songs could be heard in the restaurant, there were photos and illustrations of cars, women and actors from the 1950s hanging on the walls. Now, those were real people! Those were real cars! And we were eating borscht.

We finished it. We had to go. That's it! We definitely had to go... go to sleep.

"Sanya, so I'm thinking of moving to Moscow. Wanted to discuss that with you. What do you think, should I move?"

"Max, it's up to you. You've already decided, right?"

"No, not right, I haven't decided anything yet..."

"You only think you haven't decided. But in fact, if you're already talking about this, you'll be living here soon."

"And you think I shouldn't?"

"Max, I'm telling you, it's up to you. I won't be talking you out of it. But, while you still haven't fled, remember: over there, back home, you can still have this feeling that you can always leave... and that there is clear direction, a place to go. But you won't have this feeling here. There is nowhere else to go from here! Otherwise? Absolutely, you could move. But remember, this is the endpoint..."

"Got it! Endpoint over here, loneliness over there. Think about it, I know everything about everybody over there, half the city is made up of friends. That's exactly what makes it lonely!"

"Max, the loneliness here is something you can't even imagine. The bigger the city, the worse it is. And this is the biggest city," I said, shaking my head. "It's too big for me, Max. Way too big! I thought I'd settled down here, got everything figured out... And then I fell in love...! It's such a miracle, Max! This impossible, horrific city. It's so large! And clearly, we weren't supposed to meet here! The probability of such a meeting is close to zero. Almost zero! And yet it happened! And because it happened here, in this enormous city, it's such a miracle... And I can't handle it. I don't have enough strength... Everything here is too much!"

"But, Sanya, time runs faster here than back home. That means everything will pass faster, settle down faster. I also want to move here to make it faster... You know... So that I could heal up faster. Don't worry, time is on your side."

"I wish. Max, who the hell am I for time to be on my side? Who am I?! Don't ask me about anything, please. Who I am to give you advice? Except you know something, Max? You can live with that here."

"With what, Sanya?"

"With the knowledge that you are a nobody... Hang on," I asked Max. "Miss? Can you turn the music louder?"

"Sorry, no!"

"Miss, it's nighttime. There is barely anyone here!"

"I am sorry, we are not allowed. I can't…"

"Sorry, I understand," I stood up and came closer to where the sound was coming from. It was a song that I needed right now. I even knew the words to this song in English. I understood the chorus and nearly all the words… "Take my hand, take my life too, for I can't help…" I came up to the speaker and stopped. Sure, I was drunk, my leg hurt, and my exhaustion had crossed all thresholds, but I walked up to it firmly and stood up straight.

Max came up too. He stood to my left and listened. My eyes filled up with tears, which caused all the contours and rays of electric light to swim.

"Max, thank you for coming! I love you so much, pal! I am so tired! I can't take it anymore!"

"I you love so much too, Sanya! So much! I am tired, Sanya. And I can't it take any more either."

He hugged me by the shoulder, I tilted my head and pressed my temple to Max's forehead (he is shorter than I am). I began to sob silently, but freely. Max cried only with his eyes. The song played on for over a minute.

30

I liked what I said to Max: "Who the hell am I for time to be on my side?"

I remember when I first sensed time. I was quite young. Nine or ten. It was summer, August, and I was sitting outside in the courtyard. My parents and I were already back in my hometown from our summer vacation, but my friends still weren't. It was quiet and empty in the courtyard. The trees swayed, their leaves were large, the grass dusty and tall. It was hot. I was sitting on the bench, bored. Then I looked up at the sky. It was plainly blue, without clouds. A high summer sky. A trail left by an airplane was melting while another airplane was crossing the sky, leaving its own white trail. I lowered my eyes and proceeded to pick the bench with my finger. It felt nice to peel the paint from it. I remembered that the bench had been painted last year, also in the summer. My friends and I stood there and watched how a skinny old man was painting it and in, some magical way, it was turning from dirty-green to blue. But now I sat there and easily picked off entire sheets of already chapped and withered blue paint.

When I raised my eyes back to the sky, the airplane had already flown away and left a white trace, while the old trace had broken into pieces and nearly dissolved. I felt the passing of time… Soon, the rain showers would come, then winter, then snow will begin to melt… I realized that it was not something I liked, that it made me feel unhappy… I also understood that there was nothing I could do about it, but that it was nice to watch airplanes leave their trails.

I remembered this sharply, because it had been understood and felt by the "Me" who does not change. There, on that bench, sat the same Me who stood and listened to the song and cried. EVERYTHING else about me would change – weight, height, interests, desires… But something did not change… And it was that something that could sense time, that loved this song, that loved…

We sat a while longer, drank more tea, for some reason I never got my cola, but I no longer wanted to bother about that. Max flatly refused to come over to my place. We didn't finish the cognac, leaving a good third of the bottle, but we couldn't drink any more of it.

Then we settled our bill, left a generous tip and came outside into fresh air. We left the flashlight and the bottle on the table… Our movements resembled that of some lobster-like creatures in a fish store, still very much alive, but placed under ice and not too interested in attracting the shoppers' attention.

It had stopped snowing.

There were three cars in the parking lot, including the Mercedes. Its engine was running, the interior light was on.

"Well, Sanya, tomorrow, or actually today, I'll be sleeping till about three, if my relatives let me."

"Let's just go to my place! How long do I have to beg you? Don't be stubborn, Max."

"No, thanks. I think I've had enough of you for one day. I've had enough of today period. By the way, how much would it cost to get from here to, you know, there, where I'm staying?"

I told him what the highest possible rate could be. Max nodded and shook my hand.

"Bye, Sanya," he said. "Looks like you've got a ride," he wagged his head at the Mercedes, "When I wake up, I'll call you. Stay strong…"

He walked in the direction of the Garden Ring, where it was easier to catch a taxi. I really didn't want to part with him. I had this strange feeling that we would never see each other again. Max walked slowly across the snow and I wanted to stop him, or go with him…

He took roughly twenty steps, stopped under a street light, opened his briefcase, took out a small bundle… I recognized it. It was the unfinished cigar wrapped in a paper napkin. He tossed the buddle in the snow, then fumbled inside the briefcase, closed it… Max dropped the briefcase in the snow and kept walking. He didn't throw it away, he simply unclenched his fingers, the briefcase dropped from his hand and he headed for the roadway.

I almost went the opposite way.

It got colder. I tightly buttoned the coat and flipped the collar, then took a few steps, stopped and looked back at the Mercedes, stood there for a few seconds and went up to the car.

Looking through the windshield, I could tell that Mikhail was sleeping behind the wheel. He sat with his coat unbuttoned, his seat fully reclined. His head was tossed back, mouth slightly agape, a newspaper covered the steering wheel, reading glasses still on his nose.

I thought a bit longer and knocked on the window with my fist. He was sound asleep, I knocked harder. Mikhail jerked with his entire body, sharply sat up. It seemed he didn't immediately comprehend where he was or what was happening. In the next moment, he tore the glasses off his face and sat up like nothing happened. This was usually the way young soldiers reacted when caught asleep at their posts, or students caught asleep at a lecture, as if to say, I wasn't sleeping! It made me smile.

I knocked one more time. He lowered the window midway.

"What do you need?" He asked briskly. "What do you want now?"

"Actually, I don't need anything. I am leaving. Maxim has left already. I am getting ready to go home myself. I saw that you were sleeping, so I figured you wouldn't want to wake up here and... see us gone." I shrugged. "So I decided to wake you up, that's it. Nothing else."

Mikhail rubbed his face, drank a little mineral water from the bottle.

"Do you have any cigarettes?" He asked.

"No, I don't smoke."

He nodded.

"Get in, I'll take you home, we just have to stop on the way to fill up and buy cigarettes."

"Sorry, but I am not going with you, that's out of the question."

"Oh, don't be scared, you're still..."

"I am not scared. It's just that this all looks like... I don't know what. Think about it," I spoke very calmly, "I am going home now. I really am. If you don't believe me, you can go ahead and follow me. But it's better if you just go your own way... And cigarettes, you can buy them here. They sell them back at the restaurant, if..."

He didn't let me finish. The tinted glass went up, the interior light turned off and it was as though Mikhail just disappeared. Again, I shrugged my shoulders, turned around and headed for the avenue where I could get a taxi. I walked and walked... But nobody followed me.

FINAL CHAPTER

I got a taxi and set out across the hushed city. Hushed, as in asleep… There were hardly any lights in the windows. Saturday morning was promising Moscow a gift of silence and solitude. Snow plows were at work all over the city.

When we passed along Yakimanka, I saw a tow truck being loaded up with a disfigured vehicle… the Volvo. Shards of glass could be seen all over the roadway, along with stains from some mechanical fluid… mostly likely oil.

"It was a terrible accident," said the driver. He spoke with a thick Caucasian accent, "some five people died instantly. I almost crashed here myself. It's scary to drive nowadays. Everybody's lost their mind."

I looked at him. A neat-looking, dark-haired man of about forty. The car was filled with strongly aromatized sweet air. The driver had a large gold signet ring on his finger. I turned away. I could no longer speak. I was going home. All that I was capable of saying in one day I had already said.

The streets were desolate. Each time we stopped at a traffic light, I looked over my shoulder. No one followed. I turned to look three times and rode the rest of the way at ease. Then again, by then I was at ease regardless.

"Thank you," was all that I could muster as I paid the driver and left the car…

The moment I got home, I remembered my promise. There were still words left to say after all… I had to say them! I dialed her number… She didn't pick up right away. I woke Her up. She spoke in a horse, sleepy voice, one that was somehow unprotected.

"Hello," I said. "I am home. Everything is alright. Don't worry. Did you sleep?"

"Yes, I'd already fallen asleep."

"I am so sorry, but I just got back. So I'm calling you, as promised."

"Thank you… I was worried."

"So, should I call back in the morning?"

"Of course! But not too early."

"Alright. How about, whoever wakes up first makes the call."

"But not before twelve, alright?"

"Agreed. Can't wait, my love! I'm sorry to disturb."

"Can't wait! Till then. Till today…"

"Till today!" I said and hung up.

I said "my love" to her! I said that and didn't feel like it was a major event. I said it calmly. These words flew out of me with ease…

I turned the lights on everywhere… I left the overcoat in the hallway, tossed the jacket over the armchair, thinking: "I must not forget to shake those glassy shards from the flashlight out of my pocket…" I went to the bedroom, over to the exercise bike, to hang up the shirt. I'd already taken off the neckerchief and thought I'd hang it up there too. I was unbuttoning and walking at the same time…

There was already a shirt hanging on the exercise bike, and more than one, maybe three of them… one over another. "I should do the laundry," I thought feebly. "Sunday, I'll do it then."

I own many shirts, but there was only one left hanging in the closet, light-pink, a nice one, but the last one… I remembered looking inside the closet in the morning, there were two shirts, white and pink. I took the white one, thinking the pink would be too much… I rarely wore it, that's why it ended up being the last. "Now I'll have to wear it," I decided. What else was there to do? It was the last clean shirt I had in my house. The rest were piled in the laundry basket next to the washing machine, hanging off chairs, on the exercise bike… You can't wear a shirt for more than one day… No way. Maybe others do it, but I can't.

I stood there for a few moments, contemplating, then hung my blue neckerchief over the dirty shirts. As for the battered, filthy white shirt – I didn't even hang it up – I just threw it on the floor…

While brushing my teeth, I suddenly froze with the toothbrush in my mouth and, for some time, without any thought, studied my body reflected in the bathroom mirror down to my waist. "It's alright," I said without sound.

I almost never made my bed in the morning. "I'll change the sheets on Sunday," I decided firmly, fluffed my pillow, gave the blanket a shake, turned off the light and lay down. My body nearly drowned in delight…

The light was still on in the hallway. It was visible… At first, I thought the hell with it, but in a minute got up to turn it off. I wanted to fall asleep without aggravation…

In the hallway, I glanced at the phone on the shelf. I picked it up, stood for a bit… and dialed Max. For a while, no one answered. Finally, I heard a very sleepy and agitated woman's voice.

"Hello! Hello!" She said. "Who is it? Go ahead, speak."

"I'm sorry, may I speak with Maxim?"

"Have you lost your mind! You know what time it is?"

"Forgive me, for goodness' sake! I am his friend, I'm calling his number, worried, if he's made it or…"

"He's made it, he's made it! Where else would he be? He is right here, sleeping in his clothes. I'll have to undress him now. You woke up the whole house, not that he even cares. Go to sleep already! Everything is fine with your precious Maxim."

"Are you his aunt?" I asked out of good manners.

"No, I am his uncle! What are you asking these stupid things for? Young man, enough with this interrogation. Is this all?"

"Yes! Yes! Thank you! I am sorry, please, forgive me…"

"That's it! Goodbye."

The dial tone followed.

I lay down in bed, assumed my favorite pose, the pillow hugged my head, I glanced with one eye at the blue light overlaying the fabric of the pillowcase… it fell from the window and stretched across the pillow… I closed my eyes.

The wind grew stronger at dawn, it carried sand, and that flying sand resembled a strange fog. I even had to put on special goggles.

While Max slept, I prepared to dispatch the documents taken from the enemy along with the wounded scout. There were fourteen men left in my platoon. I ordered all of them to leave. The soldiers couldn't understand and refused to leave me… But I left an old sergeant in charge of the platoon, ordered him to deliver the important documents at any cost, explained that the wounded man would have to be carried by rotation, but that they would have to move very quickly. They had two, three hours at most until the enemy launched a pursuit.

"Besides, there is only one machine gun," I said in front of the formation. "So there is no sense in staying. You won't put up much of a fight with your rifles around here. Go on and don't think about me."

"What about the lieutenant?" The sergeant asked.

"Let him sleep some more. He decided to say. If he said so, it's useless talking him out of it, nor can I give him orders... That's it, brothers! No time for talking," I told my soldiers. "Go on! Good luck!"

"Take this, sergeant," I handed him an envelope. "This is my written order to retreat."

We embraced.

Max slept in a tent, paying no attention to how loudly it clapped in the wind. I let him sleep some more, then woke him up. We brewed coffee from the remaining water and a fistful of grounds. It came out strong.

We drank the coffee in silence, then I poured the whiskey in two small matching tin cups... We lit up cigars and enjoyed the whiskey for five minutes or so. When the whiskey was gone, we went to the machine gun. The wind was blowing at the tiny embers from our cigars and instantly carrying away the smoke.

The flag was beating away at the mast.

There were only three centimeters left of my cigar when, through the veil of sand, we saw shadows of the advancing force. They were coming closer. I aimed the machine gun at them. It was somehow eerie to take that first shot. Max tapped me on the shoulder, I looked at him, he was also finishing his cigar, holding the butt in the left corner of his mouth. He was smiling. Max winked at me, snapped his rifle, raised it and aimed busily, then pulled the trigger. One silhouette fell. Then I pressed the trigger of the machine gun...

At once, the attackers began to shoot. Bullets whistled. Some pierced the sand bags, some flew very closely by... We were shooting... Max, infrequently, with aim and precision, I in short bursts...

My soldiers, those who were leaving... could perhaps hear sporadic shooting for some time, and amid this confusion one could make out dry shots of Max's rifle and the buzzing bursts of my machine gun. They might have heard this for some time if the wind carried the sound of battle far enough... There had to be somebody to hear it...

A Brown Man in Russia
Lessons Learned on the Trans-Siberian
by Vijay Menon

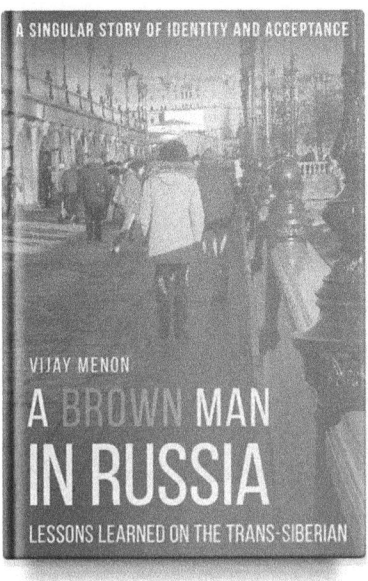

A Brown Man in Russia describes the fantastical travels of a young, colored American traveler as he backpacks across Russia in the middle of winter via the Trans-Siberian. The book is a hybrid between the curmudgeonly travelogues of Paul Theroux and the philosophical works of Robert Pirsig. Styled in the vein of Hofstadter, the author lays out a series of absurd, but true stories followed by a deeper rumination on what they mean and why they matter. Each chapter presents a vivid anecdote from the perspective of the fumbling traveler and concludes with a deeper lesson to be gleaned. For those who recognize the discordant nature of our world in a time ripe for demagoguery and for those who want to make it better, the book is an all too welcome antidote. It explores the current global climate of despair over differences and outputs a very different message – one of hope and shared understanding. At times surreal, at times inappropriate, at times hilarious, and at times deeply human, A Brown Man in Russia is a reminder to those who feel marginalized, hopeless, or endlessly divided that harmony is achievable even in the most unlikely of places.

Buy it > www.glagoslav.com

Little Zinnobers
by Elena Chizhova

Is it possible to cultivate fundamental human values if you live in a totalitarian state? A teacher who instigates the school theatre sets out to prove that it is. But while the pupils rehearse Shakespeare's tragedies and comedies under her ever-vigilant eye, Soviet life makes its brutal adjustments. This can be called a book about love, the tough kind of love that gets you through life, and death.

Zinnobers is especially fascinating for British readers as we see Shakespeare's famous sonnets and plays are touchingly brought to life by the Russian children and their gifted teacher, the novel's heroine. The teacher applies some of the playwright's satire to the socio-political situation of the USSR, using her English lessons to teach her students life's broader lessons, too.

Echoes of the Soviet Union can be felt in our own society today: the people find themselves increasingly at odds with the politicians' hypocrisy, 'big brother' is watching us through thousands of CCTVs, and political correctness determines what we can and cannot say...

Buy it > www.glagoslav.com

Leo Tolstoy – Flight from Paradise

by Pavel Basinsky

Over a hundred years ago, something truly outrageous occurred at Yasnaya Polyana. Count Leo Tolstoy, a famous author aged eighty-two at the time, took off, destination unknown. Since then, the circumstances surrounding the writer's whereabouts during his final days and his eventual death have given rise to many myths and legends. In this book, popular Russian writer and reporter Pavel Basinsky delves into the archives and presents his interpretation of the situation prior to Leo Tolstoy's mysterious disappearance. Basinsky follows Leo Tolstoy throughout his life, right up to his final moments. Reconstructing the story from historical documents, he creates a visionary account of the events that led to the Tolstoys' family drama.

Flight from Paradise will be of particular interest to international researchers studying Leo Tolstoy's life and works, and is highly recommended to a broader audience worldwide.

Buy it > www.glagoslav.com

TIME OF THE OCTOPUS

by Anatoly Kucherena

A frightening, prophetic vision of our world...

In Moscow's Sheremetyevo airport, fugitive US intelligence officer Joshua Kold is held in limbo, unable to leave the airport's transit area. He is on the run, after blowing the lid off the terrifying reach of covert American global surveillance operations. Will the Russian authorities grant him asylum, or will they hand him over the clutches of the global octopus eager for revenge for his betrayal?

As this gripping psychological and political thriller unfolds, a Moscow lawyer takes Kold to a secret bunker and grills him intently on just why he did it. Upon Kold's answers hang not only his own fate, but much, much more as the true extent of this chilling 1984 world unfolds.

Anatoly Kucherena is the famous Russian lawyer who took on the case of the American whistleblower Edward Snowden whose revelations about US intelligence operations sent shockwaves around the world in 2013. Time of the Octopus is a fiction, but it is based on Kucherena's own interviews with Snowden at Sheremetyevo, and provides the basis for Oliver Stone's major Hollywood movie 'Snowden' starring Joseph Gordon-Levitt, one of the movie events of 2016...

Buy it > www.glagoslav.com

Death of the Snake Catcher

by Ak Welsapar

This book features people from one of the most closed countries of today's world, where the passage of time resembles the passage of a caravan through the waterless desert. This world has been recreated by a true-born son of that mysterious country, a Turkmen who, at the will of fate, has now been living for a quarter of a century in snowy Scandinavia. Is that not why two different worlds come together in *Ryazan horseradish and Tula gingerbread*, to come apart in *Love in Lilac*, in which a student from the non-free world falls in love with a girl from the West?

In the story *Death of the Snake Catcher*, an old snake catcher meets one on one with a giant cobra in the heart of the desert. In the dialogue between them the author unveils the age-old interdependence of Man and untamed nature, where the fear and mistrust of the strong and the hopes and apprehensions of the weak change places but co-exist as ever. *Egyptian night of fear*, in which a boy goes to an Eastern bazaar and falls into the clutches of depraved forces, is created in the writer's characteristic style of magical realism, while the novella Altynai celebrates first love, radiant and sad, pure as virgin snow.

Buy it > www.glagoslav.com

One-Two

by Igor Eliseev

Two conjoined babies are born at the crossroads of two social worldviews. Girls are named Faith and Hope. After spending their childhood in a foster home and obtaining primary education, they understand that they are different from other people in many respects. The problems of their growing up are exacerbated with permanent humiliations from society.

Finally, fortune favors them, slightly opening a door to happiness – separation surgery that theoretically can be performed in the capital. And sisters start their way, full of difficulties and obstacles. Will they be able to overcome a wall of public cynicism together with internal conflicts among themselves? Will they find a justification for their existence and accept it? Searching for the answers to these and many other questions constitutes the essence of this novel...

Buy it > www.glagoslav.com

Glagoslav Publications Catalogue

- *The Time of Women* by Elena Chizhova
- *Andrei Tarkovsky: The Collector of Dreams* by Layla Alexander-Garrett
- *Andrei Tarkovsky - A Life on the Cross* by Lyudmila Boyadzhieva
- *Sin* by Zakhar Prilepin
- *Hardly Ever Otherwise* by Maria Matios
- *Khatyn* by Ales Adamovich
- *The Lost Button* by Irene Rozdobudko
- *Christened with Crosses* by Eduard Kochergin
- *The Vital Needs of the Dead* by Igor Sakhnovsky
- *The Sarabande of Sara's Band* by Larysa Denysenko
- *A Poet and Bin Laden* by Hamid Ismailov
- *Watching The Russians (Dutch Edition)* by Maria Konyukova
- *Kobzar* by Taras Shevchenko
- *The Stone Bridge* by Alexander Terekhov
- *Moryak* by Lee Mandel
- *King Stakh's Wild Hunt* by Uladzimir Karatkevich
- *The Hawks of Peace* by Dmitry Rogozin
- *Harlequin's Costume* by Leonid Yuzefovich
- *Depeche Mode* by Serhii Zhadan
- *The Grand Slam and other stories (Dutch Edition)* by Leonid Andreev
- *METRO 2033 (Dutch Edition)* by Dmitry Glukhovsky
- *METRO 2034 (Dutch Edition)* by Dmitry Glukhovsky
- *A Russian Story* by Eugenia Kononenko
- *Herstories, An Anthology of New Ukrainian Women Prose Writers*
- *The Battle of the Sexes Russian Style* by Nadezhda Ptushkina
- *A Book Without Photographs* by Sergey Shargunov
- *Down Among The Fishes* by Natalka Babina
- *disUNITY* by Anatoly Kudryavitsky
- *Sankya* by Zakhar Prilepin
- *Wolf Messing* by Tatiana Lungin
- *Good Stalin* by Victor Erofeyev
- *Solar Plexus* by Rustam Ibragimbekov

- *The Garden of Divine Songs and Collected Poetry of Hryhory Skovoroda*
- *Adventures in the Slavic Kitchen: A Book of Essays with Recipes*
- *Seven Signs of the Lion* by Michael M. Naydan
- *Forefathers' Eve* by Adam Mickiewicz
- *One-Two* by Igor Eliseev
- *Girls, be Good* by Bojan Babić
- *Time of the Octopus* by Anatoly Kucherena
- *The Grand Harmony* by Bohdan Ihor Antonych
- *The Selected Lyric Poetry Of Maksym Rylsky*
- *The Shining Light* by Galymkair Mutanov
- *The Frontier: 28 Contemporary Ukrainian Poets - An Anthology*
- *Acropolis - The Wawel Plays* by Stanisław Wyspiański
- *Contours of the City* by Attyla Mohylny
- *Conversations Before Silence: The Selected Poetry of Oles Ilchenko*
- *The Secret History of my Sojourn in Russia* by Jaroslav HašekCharles S. Kraszewski
- *Mirror Sand - An Anthology of Russian Short Poems in English Translation* (A Bilingual Edition)
- *Maybe We're Leaving* by Jan Balaban
- *Death of the Snake Catcher* by Ak WelsaparRichard Govett
- *A Brown Man in Russia - Perambulations Through A Siberian Winter* by Vijay Menon
- *Hard Times* by Ostap Vyshnia
- *The Flying Dutchman* by Anatoly Kudryavitsky
- *Nikolai Gumilev's Africa* by Nikolai Gumilev
- *Combustions* by Srđan Srdić
- *The Sonnets* by Adam Mickiewicz
- *Dramatic Works* by Zygmunt Krasiński
- *Four Plays* by Juliusz Słowacki
- *Little Zinnobers* by Elena Chizhova
- *A Flame Out at Sea* by Dmitry Novikov
- *We Are Building Capitalism! Moscow in Transition 1992-1997*
- *The Nuremberg Trials* by Alexander Zvyagintsev
- *Duel* by Borys Antonenko-Davydovych
- *Mikhail Bulgakov: The Life and Times* by Marietta Chudakova

More coming soon...